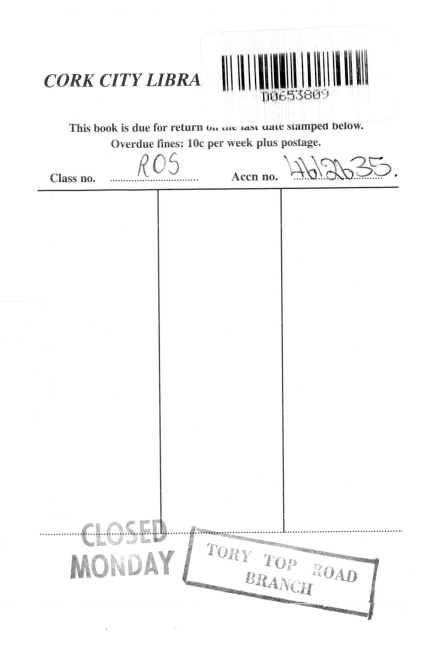

Shorecliff

Shorecliff

Marilyn Ross

THORNDIKE
CHIVERS

This Large Print edition is published by Thorndike Press®,
Waterville, Maine USA and by BBC Audiobooks, Ltd,
Bath, England.

Published in 2003 in the U.S. by arrangement with
Maureen Moran Agency.

Published in 2003 in the U.K. by arrangement with
the author.

U.S. Hardcover 0-7862-6085-8 (Romance)
U.K. Hardcover 0-7540-7771-3 (Chivers Large Print)
U.K. Softcover 0-7540-7772-1 (Camden Large Print)

The text of this Large Print edition is unabridged.
Other aspects of the book may vary from the original edition.

Set in 16 pt. Plantin.

Printed in the United States on permanent paper.

British Library Cataloguing-in-Publication Data available

Library of Congress Cataloging-in-Publication Data

Ross, Marilyn, 1912–
    Shorecliff / Marilyn Ross.
        p. cm.
    ISBN 0-7862-6085-8 (lg. print : hc : alk. paper)
    1. Inheritance and succession — Fiction.   2. Women
murderers — Fiction.   3. Married people — Fiction.
4. Haunted houses — Fiction.   5. Large type books.
I. Title.
PR9199.3.R5996S56 2003
                                        2003065082

To my Aunt Tillie
— Mrs. Aubrey H. McDonald

CHAPTER ONE

Sometimes in the stillness of the night Anita Shore would suddenly awake, raise herself on her elbow and stare into the darkness with alarm. Perhaps her sleep had been disturbed by the harsh cry of a night bird, the nocturnal creaking of the old mansion known as Shorecliff, or merely the strong ocean breeze buffeting an ancient shutter. After a long moment she would realize she was awakened by some mundane thing, rather than the haunting terror that had plagued her for months when she first came to the brooding white and green clapboard house.

Yet in the middle of the night that other time seemed terrifyingly vivid and visions of the supernatural world would always lurk in her subconscious. An eerie screeching cry, the unexpected moan of a floorboard, or the sighing of a night wind often were all that were necessary to fire her imagination, to bring back the memory of a perfect expressionless beauty floating close to her in the shrouded velvet darkness; of the touch of cold, limp fingers of the long dead reaching out to caress her own warm flesh. Such sounds revived memories of an evil beauty, buried for decades in the family cemetery, who had returned from the grave to jealously cherish the husband Anita loved, to dominate him with a perverse charm that had survived death — and turn him into a sullen, obsessed stranger.

Anita scorned the spirit world until she came to Shorecliff, but would never dare dismiss such things casually again. She had learned her lesson well. She had come to know the menace of earthbound spirits. She had seen the face and figure of corrupt ghostly loveliness moving with haunting grace along the shadowed corridors of Shorecliff and standing on the high bluff staring sadly out toward sea. Anita learned the dark, tragic history of the long dead enchantress and she had summoned the strength to battle the spell that had been cast over the ancient house and her husband. And yet in the silence of the night she still feared her!

It really began on that June afternoon when they left Boston for Shorecliff.

They had been married only three months. It was a perfect three months for Anita. She continued working for the law firm that had employed her since she graduated from a Providence business college and came to Boston, but neither her busy days at the office nor the fact that her husband, Charles, was still convalescing from a serious motor accident of a year before, stopped her from enjoying those peaceful early days of marriage. She reveled in the new role of wife and homemaker in their tiny apartment on Beacon Hill.

Perhaps it was the mere fact that Charles had survived the head-on collision which had taken two lives that induced the heightened glow of happiness. She had gone through those lonely, frightening hours of waiting in hospital corridors to learn whether he would live another day. So when he began his recovery it seemed nothing so terrifying could threaten their happiness again. She was naive then — and had not set foot in Shorecliff.

But letters had come from the old house by the sea in New Hampshire — four or five of them with the postmark Pennbridge and the neat, fine penmanship of an earlier day. Charles explained these letters were from his Aunt Clare. He had spent a number of summers with the elderly woman as a child but there had been a quarrel between her and his mother and so he had not visited New Hampshire for many years. Nor had his Aunt Clare shown the slightest sign of wanting him to — until she read of his accident. Then she wrote sympathetically and at length. She invited him to see her and had spoken of her own poor health.

Charles made a slow recovery from the serious head injuries he'd suffered in the smash-up. And so he did little traveling up to the time of their marriage. In fact he only returned to his position as a reporter on the Boston Globe about a month before the wedding. So he didn't get down to New Hampshire but he did ask Anita to send his Aunt an invitation to the wedding. Anita was happy to do this since she had hardly any relatives of her own. Except for some young friends, there would be few guests for the ceremony.

Aunt Clare wrote a polite note explaining she was not well enough to attend the wedding. She also sent them a present. A handsome antique silver tray.

They had set their gifts out on a table in the living room of their new apartment. And when Anita unwrapped the huge tray her blue eyes opened wide with surprise.

"This is a fabulous present!" she exclaimed, holding it for Charles to see. "Your Aunt Clare must be very wealthy."

Charles was lounging in an easy chair near the table. His thin, sensitive face showed amusement. "She has enough," he said in his usual quiet way. He had always been shy and withdrawn and Anita noticed this was even more pronounced since his accident. Sometimes it worried her and she wondered if the injury had left him neurotic.

Anita placed the tray prominently on the table with the other presents. "I wish she was able to come to the wedding," she said. "We must send her a special thank you note. This is our most valuable present."

"When Aunt Clare does anything she usually does it well," Charles said.

Anita turned to him with a questioning look. There were times when she resented his taciturn disposition. She really knew very little about him or his people. Their personalities were very different. She was blonde, outgoing, and attractive, with a knack for making friends. She had a slim but sturdy figure and excelled in swimming and skiing. Charles was dark and slender, sensitive and quiet and did not fit the usual stereotype of a newspaper reporter. Actually he wasn't pleased with his choice of profession. His one ambition was to gain enough financial independence to become a free-lance writer.

Anita said, "You've hardly told me anything about your family."

He smiled, and he had such a warm smile that it always reassured her doubts, as he said, "There's not much family left. Just Aunt Clare and the adopted daughter who stays with her. And Aunt Clementine who lives in the other part of the family home."

"The other part?" she asked, not understanding.

He nodded. "Yes. You see Shorecliff was built by two brothers long ago. It is a twin house with two complete sections. Both houses have a common wall but aside from that they have separate front and rear entrances, cellars and garages."

"That's rather unusual."

"Not as unusual as you'd think," Charles assured her. "Many of the old New England houses had built-on wings housing separate families. In this case the two houses are exactly alike. Neither brother wanted the other to get ahead of him."

12

"What about this adopted daughter who lives with your Aunt Clare?" Anita wanted to know.

"She's about your own age," he said. "I've never seen her in person but I've had snapshots of her. She's pretty and intelligent looking. I gather she's very devoted to Aunt Clare. She'll likely inherit her section of the house and her money eventually. Her name is Patricia."

"Lucky girl!" Anita commented without being in the least envious.

But it was to turn out that the attractive Patricia wasn't quite all that lucky. The news came to Anita one day in late May. Charles phoned her from his office at noon as he often did.

"Can you meet me for lunch at one-thirty?" he asked.

She checked her desk clock and saw that it was close to one o'clock. "I don't know," she hesitated. "I have a lot of work to finish and it's almost one now."

"Leave the work," he said. "I have some special news."

"All right. Where?"

"Parker House Grill," he said. "That's the nearest place for you. I'll meet you in the hotel lobby about one-thirty five."

He was waiting for her in the elegant,

paneled lobby. She thought he looked especially elated and after they were seated at their table in the grill room, she asked, "Well, what's on your mind?"

"We're rich," he informed her across the table.

She returned his smile. "In happiness, yes."

"No!" he protested. "I mean we really are rich."

Anita stared at him in astonishment. "Go on! You fascinate me!"

"Aunt Clare died a couple of weeks ago. Her Boston lawyers have just been in touch with me. She left me her house and the major share of her estate."

"Charles!"

"It's true."

She swallowed hard, trying to take it in, to understand what it would mean to them, to Charles who was working again even though he was far from well. She said, "Is it really a lot of money?"

"Several hundred thousand dollars," Charles said happily. "Plus the house. And it's worth a good deal."

"That's a fantastic sum for people like us," Anita told him.

"Sure is. It means we can both quit our jobs and I can settle down to writing that novel I've always wanted to do."

"I still can't believe it!" she sighed.

He laughed. "Good old Aunt Clare. She sure fooled me. I thought Patricia was going to get it all."

Anita remembered. "Her adopted daughter! Of course! Surely she didn't ignore her in the will?"

"No. But I don't think she's getting as much as she expected. Aunt Clare left her a trust fund of a hundred thousand dollars and the right to go on living at Shorecliff as long as she likes."

"Then she really got the house, not us."

"No," Charles shook his head. "Patricia may live there but the house is ours. I think Aunt Clare wanted to be sure she didn't have to go on living there alone."

A baffled expression crossed Anita's face. "You're seriously considering living there in the same house with that girl?"

"Why not? It's a large house."

She frowned. "Have you thought about what the girl's feelings may be? This Patricia may resent our moving in on her. Especially since you've been left the lion's share of her foster parent's money."

"I don't think so," Charles said. "From what I've learned about her she is a pleasant person. Not one apt to hold a grudge."

15

Anita studied his glowing face and thought that just hearing this news had made him look better than she'd seen him in weeks. She didn't have the heart to keep denigrating their good fortune even if she had some serious doubts about the legacy.

She contented herself by saying, "We are very happy now. And I like our tiny apartment. Do you think this money will bring us so much more?"

"It will give me the chance to do my novel," he smiled. "That's my main interest just now." He paused. "So when you go back to the office be sure to give notice."

"I hate to do that," she said. "Burning our bridges."

"We have the money. There's no question about it. We have to begin a different kind of life," he told her. "So don't worry about a small thing like your job."

"It's been mighty important to us that I've worked up until now," she said. "I'll feel terrible when I tell them."

"Has to be done," he said. "I'm handing in my resignation. And we'll be leaving for Shorecliff in two weeks."

"That soon?"

"Yes. Aunt Clare wanted me to take up residence there as soon as possible."

"What about your Aunt Clementine and your cousin Gordon?"

"They won't bother us any. They're in their own house."

"But you said it was part of the main building. That they are twin houses."

"So they are," he agreed. "But Aunt Clementine and Gordon keep to themselves."

"Are they as wealthy as your Aunt Clare was?"

He shook his head. "I think not. But they must be reasonably well off. Aunt Clem's husband sold the rights in his lumber business before his death. Her son, Gordon, is a Harvard graduate in arts. And he makes his living operating an antique shop in Pennbridge."

She smiled. "Sounds like a gentleman's profession."

"He's an only son and has stayed close to his mother."

"And never married?"

"No. I have an idea Aunt Clementine is a possessive type." He paused to smile again. "You'll like New Hampshire. And we'll be going down there at a good time of year."

Anita nodded. "You spent a lot of summers there as a boy."

17

"Yes. Gordon and I used to play together and fight like tinkers. Aunt Clem was forever warning Aunt Clare that I'd turn out to be a ruffian."

Anita looked at him fondly. "And so you have! An adorable ruffian!"

"I hope Aunt Clem agrees with you," he said. "Anyway it's not likely Gordon and I are liable to get in any brawls these days."

"And if you do we can always come back to Boston," she said.

He studied her with a searching glance. "You don't sound enthusiastic about becoming an heiress," he said. "You don't seem to relish the idea of going down to Shorecliff to live."

"I'm not sure I've digested it all yet," she said with a rueful smile. "And then the idea of sharing the house with that girl isn't too appealing."

"The house is so large you'll never notice she's around," he promised. "And you'll have a housekeeper, a maid and a handyman and gardener. You're going to be a young woman of importance."

"Will I measure up to it?" she wondered. And she really was worried. She had a modest background — orphaned before she was ten and reared by a childless married aunt in Providence. Being mistress of a large house would present her with a whole new set of problems.

Charles must have read her thoughts for he assured her, "You won't be burdened with a lot of household details right away. Patricia has been looking after the house and she'll probably be glad to go on doing so."

She gave him a faint smile. "It sounds as if I'm not only giving up my job but retiring as well!"

"Don't you worry about finding things to do," he said. "I'll need someone to type my manuscript and we can begin to think about that family we've planned."

So it all sounded promising enough. She tried to convince herself they were unbelievably lucky. Yet she left her job with misgivings and with no bright hopes for the future and packed her things in the apartment in which they'd been so happy.

Perhaps, if she'd been less considerate of Charles, she would have spoken out frankly and told him she felt she was trading their happy apartment for a new home that really wouldn't be hers. But she kept silent because he was so enthusiastic about moving to Shorecliff. And there was another side to it. She was jealous of Patricia Shore, sight unseen. She couldn't help but be. The idea of sharing much of her time with Charles with another attractive young woman was one she didn't relish. Even though this Patricia might be a paragon of virtue it was a lot to ask. She didn't think Aunt Clare had been so generous after all, expecting them all to live together in this fashion.

They sent their furniture ahead in a moving van and drove down to Shorecliff in their own car, a sporty British convertible. They reached the New Hampshire turnpike in less than an hour and Anita was startled to learn that the New Hampshire coastline and Pennbridge were actually so close to Boston. It was a sunny, warm afternoon as they drove along the evergreen-bordered turnpike. She sat back in the car and drew in a deep breath of the cool, pine-scented air.

Smiling lazily at Charles, she said, "I'm beginning to be convinced. This air is a whole lot fresher than in Boston."

"I told you," he said with a triumphant glance. "We're going to really begin living down here."

"It will have its advantages," she admitted. "We'll get there about four o'clock. Do you suppose Patricia has been waiting for us?"

He said, "You seem unduly worried about her."

"I don't want to get off to a bad start."

"If anyone should be worrying about that it's Patricia," Charles pointed out. "The house is ours, not hers. And she will be living there with us, not us living there with her."

Anita smiled wryly. "I doubt if she'll notice the fine distinction. She is bound to feel more at home in Shorecliff since she's lived there all these years."

Charles frowned at the wheel. "I've lived there, too. And I'm not going to allow her to make us feel uneasy."

She decided she was only upsetting him so she'd say no more. Especially because he'd been having headache attacks again. He'd suffered greatly from them in the first months after the accident. The doctors had warned her they might go on indefinitely but then they had suddenly improved. She blamed the latest attacks on his excitement about the inheritance and moving to Shorecliff. And she hoped that once they were settled he'd be better again.

Giving him a troubled glance, she said, "Do you have a headache?"

"Not really," he said with mild annoyance. "Just the hint of one."

She didn't bother him with more questions. She could tell by the lack of color in his face and his taut manner that he was having one of his spells. And she was unhappy that it should strike him at this time when they were nearing the seaside mansion they'd inherited.

They paid the toll at Hampton and took the first side road to the right. When they had driven several miles they took another branch road that was marked with a sign stating Pennbridge was five miles distant. Now they were passing comfortable farms in a strictly rural area and she could tell they were moving nearer the coast because of the increased dampness.

After some minutes they took a wider paved road that led them directly to Pennbridge. It was a typical seaside New England town with its quota of gas stations and motels on the outskirts, along with automobile dealerships and roadside eating places that looked squalid in the daylight.

Pennbridge consisted of one broad commercial street lined with all the main business places and the post office, the courthouse and the public library. A number of tree-lined side streets comprised the residential area. And she saw there were some very fine old homes. Many had the dates when they'd been built over the front doorways; some went back to the late 1790's. She had an idea Shorecliff was almost that old.

Charles drove down a short section of the main street and then turned right again to an elm-shaded street heading straight to the shore, past some large old homes with white picket fences and an occasional colorful sign of an artist's studio or the small building of some commercial establishment. Anita saw a barn-like white structure set in a distance off the street. A bizarre sampling of old tables and chairs were set out in front of it along with a dozen or more colored glass bottles of a gallon size. Over the top of the barn door a black and white sign announced, "G. Morehouse, Antiques."

She sat up in her seat and pointed to it. "That must be your cousin's shop."

He glanced back casually. "Yes. I'd say that was it. He does most of his business in the summer time. It's a tourist proposition. In the other seasons he scouts for furniture and repairs it."

"Are we far from Shorecliff?"

"Just a couple of miles," he said. "The next road to the left and straight down to the end."

She realized there was a thin haze of fog over the late sunny afternoon, just enough to give it a slightly bluish tinge and to make her shiver. It was some degrees cooler than on the expressway. Charles was still driving without a jacket and she worried that his short-sleeved linen shirt wasn't warm enough for him. His blue blazer was thrown in the back. He'd decided on a blazer and gray flannels for the drive down. Before the accident she'd never worried about her handsome husband but his health condition had been tricky since then.

At last they came to a gateway flanked by gray stone posts. Beyond were flat, grassy lawns and green hedges and ornamental trees. And far ahead in the middle of all the careful landscaping stood a massive white and green wooden house — or rather twin houses since the two were built as one unit, yet each had its own square observation tower, its own four story splendor with wide porches and rounded glass observatories at each end.

Charles smiled at her. "The brothers translated an Italian stone villa they once saw into this twin wooden version. And the white clapboards and green trim don't go too badly with the general style."

They drove around to the front entrance which had a rounded top in green trim. The front door was white and had inserts of frosted panes of glass. Anita noted the circular stained glass windows at the third level of the tower that rose directly from the entrance door. She was intrigued by the quaint green shutters. "It's a divine old house," she said, staring at it.

"I thought you'd like it," Charles told her as he stopped the car.

At the same moment the front door opened and a young woman appeared. She was so breathlessly lovely that the sight of her shattered Anita's confidence. Was this Patricia? The girl was wearing a short chic linen dress that did full justice to her slender, lovely body. Her brown hair was cut in the Twiggy style and her face was sensuous, with high cheek bones, large hazel eyes, a pert nose and full lips that were now set in a warm smile of greeting. Anita felt hopelessly out of it in her modest print dress.

Patricia came toward the car and held out a tanned hand set off by a white coral bracelet. "I'm Pat," she said. "Welcome to Shorecliff."

The picture of beauty was not lost on Charles. He took the brown-haired girl's hand and then moved in to touch his lips to her cheek. "Thank you, Pat," he said. And turning to Anita, guided her closer, "This is my wife, Anita."

Pat, smiling and at ease, came up and embraced her and they kissed. "I do hope you two will be happy here," she said.

"It's a lovely country," Anita said. And then to cover her awkward feeling she made a show of staring out at the ocean just beyond the front lawn. Facing the cliff, she noted the fog hovering there, and added, "Though I see you do get some fog."

"Quite a lot," Pat admitted. "I try to tell myself it's good for the complexion. It does come in every day about this time." She turned to include Charles in her conversation. "Aunt Clem and Gordon would have liked to have been here when you arrived but Gordon had to be at the shop and Aunt Clem is on the Altar Guild of the church this month and it's her afternoon at the church."

"We'll have plenty of time to see them," Charles said. "Did the van with our stuff get here?"

"It came early," Pat said. "I had several rooms emptied on the second floor and they put everything in them. Of course you needn't worry about rushing to unpack. You have plenty of completely furnished rooms including your bedroom."

"That certainly takes a lot of the pain out of moving," Anita said. She found Pat charming and liked her already.

"You must both be tired," the girl said. "Come on inside. I have some martinis waiting for you."

Charles flashed Anita a smile, as if to underline his promise that she would like Patricia and the old house. As soon as they entered the hallway Anita was aware of the rich store of fine antique furniture that the previous owners had gathered. Pat led them directly into the large living room on the left and in the subdued light of the foggy afternoon it struck Anita as having a rare mauve elegance. A number of family portraits decorated the walls; the ceiling was decorated with ornate carvings; and the fancy crystal chandeliers and gray marble fireplace were from a long-past era.

Pat went ahead to a sideboard as they seated themselves on a nearby carved cherry wood divan, which was covered in a striped crimson and white material. The crimson Persian carpet had a rich texture.

Pat came back with a glass in each hand. "I assume that everyone prefers martinis in

27

the afternoon," she said. "I hope I've not made a mistake. I can change them for anything you prefer."

Charles raised his glass, "These will do nicely." He had put on his blue blazer and tightened his cravat and looked rather handsome.

"To your happy future here," Pat said with a nod and then took a sip from her glass.

Anita said, "This is all new to me, although Charles tried to describe the house as he remembered it."

Pat turned to Charles. "That was some time ago. A good bit of furniture has been added and a new heating system installed along with other improvements."

"Aunt Clare kept the place up well," he said.

A strange expression flashed across the girl's pretty face. "Your aunt was quite feeble for the past two years," she said. "Most of the supervising of the house fell on me." She paused and took another sip from her glass before she said coolly, "Of course you know I expected she'd leave me this place."

Anita felt her cheeks burn and glanced at her husband. Charles looked slightly uncomfortable but he quickly replied, "I can well understand that. And I'm as surprised as you at the way things turned out."

"I think it was your accident," Pat said. "She worried about you a great deal after that. She was afraid your health wouldn't allow you to work again."

"For a time I doubted that it would," Charles admitted.

Pat offered them one of her scintillating smiles. "Please don't get the idea I'm angry about the will. She did leave me a nice amount of money and the privilege of remaining here. I'm quite satisfied."

Anita felt she should speak up. "It's generous of you to feel that way."

"Charles should have the house," Pat said. "He is a Shore. I think this place needs one of the blood to make it happy." She smiled. "You see I have a superstitious belief about Shorecliff. To me it has a personality."

Anita found this comment strange but was anxious to hold her own in the conversation. Fixing her glance on a portrait on the panel almost directly opposite her she said, "What a lovely woman!"

Pat's eyebrow raised a little. She stared at the painting of a woman in her twenties in a fancy blue dress of a century before. The woman had blonde hair and an oval face of great symmetry and beauty — a delicate face with perfect pink skin. But the eyes were the most striking feature of the portrait. The eyes, in contradiction to the meek loveliness of the woman's features, were hard and penetrating. They almost glared out of the painting, spoiling some of the effect.

Pat said, "Strange you should notice that one. That's Amanda Shore, a great beauty who lived in this house a hundred years ago. Many claim she was a murderess." She looked at Anita directly. "The rumor is that her spirit still haunts Shorecliff."

Charles had risen and gone across to study the portrait. "I remember hearing that story when I was a child," he said. "Aunt Clare scared Gordon and me with it."

Pat smiled bleakly. "Aunt Clare firmly believed in Amanda's evil powers."

Anita inexplicably felt a cold clamminess in the air around her. Averting her eyes from the hypnotic painting she asked Pat, "Why do you say evil powers?"

Pat shrugged. "Because she was a wicked woman, if the stories about her are true. She reveled in the attentions of many men, loved expensive clothes and the best of perfumes. Her prime favorite was Attar of

Roses. The story goes that she was much in love with a captain of one of the clipper ships that sailed to the Indies from Penn-bridge in those days. He married a girl in England and came here to tell Amanda. He wanted to ask forgiveness for his jilting her and beg her to be his new wife's friend. He vanished that night and was never seen again. Amanda claimed he left her early to go back to his ship but many people thought she was lying — that she had murdered him here and disposed of his body somehow. His disappearance is still a mystery."

Anita continued to feel strangely uneasy. "You surely don't believe the story."

Pat glanced at the portrait again. "Studying those eyes, I do. She showed no interest in her other admirers after that and became a devout church-goer. But she did continue to take a vain pride in her beauty. When the years began to take their toll she crossed the ocean to France for a popular beauty treatment of the era in which the facial skin was impregnated with enamel to form a doll-like pink porcelain mask. When she returned with this artificial covering on her face she looked younger but it was a strange eerie kind of beauty. She could never smile or show expression again as the enamel would crack if she did. And they say it is the pink-cheeked enamel face that still haunts Shorecliff."

Anita shuddered. "It's a horrible story!"

Charles looked thoughtful. "I disagree. It has always held an interest for me. I wish I could have known Amanda." He turned to gaze at the portrait once more.

Pat laughed lightly. "Perhaps you will."

He looked at her in surprise. "Why do you say that?"

"Aunt Clare claimed she saw her many times. Perhaps you may have the same luck."

"I wouldn't mind meeting a ghost that lovely," Charles said earnestly. "I'd like to write her story. That may be my novel."

Anita felt a growing panic and stood up quickly. "I'd like to go to our room and freshen up before dinner," she told Pat.

"Of course," the girl said. "Thoughtless of me to keep you here talking."

She led Anita and Charles up to the big bedroom on the second floor. It was as luxuriously furnished as the rooms below, in a period style with a broad double bed. Pat left them with the announcement that Aunt Clem and Gordon would be joining them for dinner.

Charles seemed oddly distant and occupied when Anita found herself alone with him. He went over to the window that overlooked the ocean and stared out.

Her nervousness increasing, Anita went over and stood a step behind him. She said, "Charles, I don't think we should stay here. I'm sure Pat resents us and I don't think we'll be happy."

He turned to her with a peculiar light in his eyes. "I must stay here," he said. "I intend to write her story."

"Whose story?"

"Amanda Shore's," he said. And he turned his back on her to stare out at the thickening fog.

Anita was about to exclaim out in anger against the idea but at that moment she saw what seemed like a shadow pass between them. And suddenly the air was filled with a fragrance.

A strong perfume that she recognized as Attar of Roses.

CHAPTER TWO

Dinner was well under way. The main course was finished and Mrs. Miller, the dour-faced housekeeper, was serving the ice cream. A shelf, lined with rare, old decorative plates, ran along the walls of the long, narrow room. Candelabra and gleaming silver and exquisite china decorated the table. Conversation had gone well and Anita became acquainted with Clementine Morehouse and her son, Gordon.

Anita had taken an instant dislike to Aunt Clem, a woman of sixty-odd years with the pinched, wrinkled face of a fanatic and a mordant tongue. Her hair was yellowish-white and tautly drawn back from a high forehead and to complete the unprepossessing picture she had rabbit teeth and spoke in a nasal, high-pitched voice. She seemed to enjoy complaining, especially about her son.

Gordon, the long-suffering son, was a mild man in his mid-thirties whose fine, attractive features were marred only by his thick-lensed horn-rimmed glasses. He was small in stature and had the Shore charm which was lacking in his mother. He had black hair and sallow skin and a habit of occasionally clasping his hands in front of him in an almost servile attitude. Anita guessed he had picked this up through interviewing and listening to long dull comments by customers when his mind was somewhere else. Anita felt sorry for Gordon and enjoyed his talk.

The thing that worried Anita most was the strange mood that had come over Charles since arriving at Shorecliff. He suddenly acted distracted and aloof. She recalled his headache during the drive from Boston and began to wonder if his old injury was going to give him further trouble. He only joined in the conversation occasionally and then his remarks were disjointed and at random, almost as if he weren't paying any attention to what was being said.

Anita was glad when dinner ended and they all moved into the living room. But her relief was short-lived for she found herself singled out by Aunt Clem. The old woman's pinched face wore a belligerent look.

"Do you think your husband is entirely recovered from his accident?" was her opener.

Anita tried hard to curb the annoyance she felt. "The doctors seem very satisfied with his condition."

"Doctors!" Aunt Clem's lip curled to reveal more of the ugly rabbit teeth. "I have no faith in them at all."

Anita smiled indulgently. "When one has head wounds such as Charles received in that accident there is no choice. Only a doctor can help."

"More's the pity!" Aunt Clem commented. "Who was to blame for the accident? Charles?"

"No," Anita said quickly. "It was completely unavoidable. Something went wrong with the steering of the other car."

This gave Aunt Clem a new subject to complain about. "They don't build anything right anymore." And she launched into a long story about a refrigerator she'd bought and which had never worked properly. "And it never will," she finished. "It wasn't put together properly at the factory."

"I know this does happen," Anita agreed.

Aunt Clem scowled viciously at Gordon, who was standing talking to Charles and

Pat. "Charles seems very nervous and edgy to me. I'd be worried about him if I were in your place."

"I think being down here will do him good," Anita suggested.

"Don't count on it," Aunt Clem said gloomily and nodded toward the window. "Look at the fog out there tonight. And this afternoon we had sunshine! The weather here can't be depended on. If Gordon had the same ambition his father had I wouldn't stay here a moment. But I may as well admit it, my son is a failure."

"He has his own antique business," Anita pointed out.

"Only because I've footed the bills for his losses," Aunt Clem said, her blue eyes snapping angrily. "He has extravagant tastes and no proper business judgment."

"I imagine there is a gamble in buying antiques, the same as in anything else," she said.

"Not if you're sharp," Aunt Clem retorted. "And Gordon is not sharp. He's the quiet, easy-going sort they put it all over on. To make it worse I think he has an eye on Patricia and he can't even support himself."

"Perhaps if he married it would change him."

"Make him worse," was the old woman's grim opinion. "No. Nothing will change Gordon." With an abrupt switch of subject she asked in the next breath, "Do you think you'll like it here?"

"I haven't had time to decide," she said.

"From the state Charles is in I'd say it would be wise to allow him to stay here and rest a little. You mark my words, that young man is on the verge of a mental breakdown. I can see it in his manner."

"He's more nervous than usual tonight," Anita admitted. "But I will stay on here if it seems to do him good."

The old woman's white face showed a bitter smile. "I'm a Shore and so I shouldn't say it but there's a streak of madness in our family that shows up every now and then. It's been a pattern through the years that every so often insanity shows up. Some mild, ordinary member of the family suddenly commits a brutal murder or does some other awful thing. I think it goes all the way back to Amanda. They say she was quite mad in her final years."

"That's her portrait, I believe," Anita said, indicating the painting. "I've heard some things about her."

"About her ghost, I'm sure," Aunt Clem

said with an all-knowing nod. "You'll be easier in mind if you shut your ears to such talk."

Anita gave her a sharp glance. "You don't believe in ghosts, then?"

The pinched, white face showed caution. "I wouldn't go as far as all that," she said. "But then I didn't subscribe to the goings on of Clare and that Mary Vane."

"Mary Vane?"

"The medium from Boston whom Clare brought down here," Aunt Clem said with a hint of anger. "Clare had too much money for her own good. She needed to find ways to get rid of it. Mary Vane was one answer."

"You talk as if you think the medium was a fake."

"Well, I don't," was Aunt Clem's nettled reply. "Mary Vane does have powers but I don't believe for a moment she was putting them to work for Clare's benefit. Though one night I attended a seance here and it made my flesh crawl."

"What happened?"

The old woman sighed. "They were trying to contact the spirit of Amanda. Clare was always anxious to clear up the mystery about that murder. Well, Mary Vane's spirit voice came through to us. I could see a blur of ectoplasm in the air. Like a shadow."

"Like a shadow?" Anita asked, startled by the remembrance of her own experience just a short while ago.

Aunt Clem nodded. "Yes, like the quick movement of a shadow. And then the room was filled with the Attar of Roses perfume. It was her favorite, you know. That was enough for me. I called Gordon and we went back to our own half of the house."

"It's an interesting story," she said. "Though it may not mean much."

"I know exactly what it meant," Aunt Clem snapped. "Amanda's soul is still unhappy and earthbound."

"Yet you didn't approve of the seances?"

"Not the wholesale way Mary Vane put them on. Every night and on many an afternoon as well. It wasn't healthy and I told them so. But Clare would never listen to anything." With that the old woman moved on to start arguing with Pat about something she insisted the girl had neglected to do.

As this harangue was going on Gordon Morehouse detached himself from the group and made his way over to her. He smiled apologetically and the eyes behind the thick-lensed glasses fixed on her with surprising sharpness.

"I gather that Mother warned you about me," he said.

Anita was astonished. "Not really. We were talking about many things."

"Mother never loses a chance to tell people what a failure I am and to complain of my lack of filial affection."

"I'm sure she can have no complaints on that score."

The young man looked sorrowful. "I like to think so but there are times when she shakes my conviction."

"Do you enjoy the antique business?"

"It's my whole life," he replied frankly. "Do you know anything about antiques?"

"No. But I'd like to learn."

"You're intelligent," he said. "It wouldn't take you long."

"Thanks," she said. "I must visit your shop."

He nodded. "Love to have you. But make sure to clear it with Charles first."

"Why?"

"Charles might misinterpret your interest in my place," he said, his eyes bright with a mocking gleam.

"Why do you say that?"

He glanced across where Charles was standing with Aunt Clem and Pat, and then turning to her, continued, "I remember his jealousy from the old days. He was always suspicious of me. We had an awful battle one time over a girl in pigtails. I don't want to ever see it repeated."

Anita was forced to smile. "And you actually think he mightn't trust me with you?"

"The idea comes to mind," Gordon Morehouse said.

"You're wrong. Charles is not the violent type."

"He was when he was younger," Gordon insisted. "Just how well do you know him?"

She smiled wryly. "I'm his wife."

"Granted, that is true," Gordon agreed. "But I have an idea that during his courting and probably in these early months of married life he's presented his best side to you. You may find him changing from now on."

The logic of it filled her with a mild panic. For Charles had certainly behaved differently since entering Shorecliff — almost as if those old memories had taken hold of him and altered his personality.

She said, "He's tired tonight. And he's never really recovered from that accident."

The eyes behind the glasses had a hypnotic look as they met hers. "I would watch him closely if I were you. And don't ever upset him. He might surprise you by his reaction."

"Nothing you have said alarms me," she promised him.

"Spoken like a good and faithful wife," Gordon said, approval in his tone. "But you should also protect yourself. I hope you'll think of me as your friend."

"I'd like to," Anita said. "It will take me some time to adjust here."

"Granted," he said. "Don't let Mother unduly upset you. Her gossip is worse than her good heart."

"I'll remember that," she smiled.

"It's a shame to shut anyone as young and lovely as you up in a place like this," he said.

"Pat has lived here for a long time."

"Pat!" Gordon grimaced. "She's a different case altogether. She was sure that Aunt Clare would leave her everything."

"She certainly doesn't seem disgruntled," Anita said.

Gordon offered her a sly smile. "And don't judge too much by appearances," he advised. "That can be dangerous, too."

She frowned. "You're telling me that Pat is two-faced."

"I'm saying that she is an average person. With an average person's aversion to being done out of a large amount of money."

"We haven't done her out of anything," Anita protested. "No one was more surprised than Charles when he heard about his aunt's will."

"No one except possibly Pat," he said cynically. "You should learn to look out for the other person's point of view."

"She seems to be doing all she can to make it pleasant for us here," Anita pointed out.

"She has made an impressive opening," Gordon admitted. "I'll be more convinced when I see what happens later on."

"You're one of the most pessimistic young men I've ever met," Anita said with some amazement.

"One gets introverted in a small place like this."

"If you don't like it you should leave."

"I don't like the place but I'm in love with my shop," he said frankly. "I don't think I could find one like it in any of the cities. So I stay here."

"Well, I appreciate your offer of help," she said. "It's good to have at least someone on my team."

"I see Charles giving us an ugly eye," Gordon told her suavely. "I guess we'd better join the others." And they did.

Pat was saying, "I think Amanda might be too deep a subject for your novel, Charles. You should try some lighter story first."

Charles shook his head. "I disagree. I think I can make this story vital enough without all the gruesome details."

"You'll find a wealth of material here in the family library," Aunt Clem said in her high-pitched voice. "Clare carefully preserved all the family records."

Charles showed interest. "I believe Aunt Clare would want me to write Amanda's story. She was always interested in it herself."

"Aunt Clare was a bit of a nut," said Gordon with amused tolerance. "She went through life believing in ghosts and evil spirits. You won't find the book-buying public so gullible."

"Exactly my thought," Pat agreed.

"I disagree," Charles objected. "I know that things with a mystic angle have great appeal."

Aunt Clem piped up, "If you want your subject matter authentic there's one sure way to get it."

"Oh?" Charles said. "And how is that?"

"Invite Mary Vane down here. She'll be glad to hold some seances. And she'll have Amanda talking to you as she had her talking to Clare when she was here last."

Charles frowned. "This medium actually claimed to have contacted Amanda?"

Another surge of panic went through Anita as she heard the tense note in her husband's voice. And she was upset because he seemed to actually accept such a spirit contact as possible. If he continued in his obsession with the dead murderess where would it lead?

Aunt Clem said, "Mary Vane gave us messages from Amanda more than once."

Pat looked disgusted. "You didn't believe in that mumbo-jumbo!"

The older woman snapped, "I'm not like some people. I accept that there is still some unexplained mystery in life."

Pat's pretty face crimsoned. "I'm not the pure cynic you try to make me. Nor am I a skeptic. But Mary Vane is a professional spiritualist. I think she'd be willing to summon any ghost at any time for a fee."

Gordon's eyes twinkled. "On the other hand I don't think we should discount all professional spiritualists as fakes. A lot of them have managed awe-inspiring feats and no one has been able to prove that trickery was used." Anita could tell that the quiet young man was deliberately baiting the others and enjoying it.

Aunt Clem gave her son her first approving look all evening. "A good point, Gordon," she said in her high-pitched fashion. "No one has been able to explain the automatic writing of Mrs. Curran. And her guide from the other land was a seventeenth-century English spinster called Patience Worth."

"I remember reading about Mrs. Curran," Charles agreed. "She lived in this country."

"That is quite correct," Aunt Clem said with a satisfied smile. "And yet she was able to write historical novels of Elizabethan England in great detail without any research. She was introduced to spirit-writing as a parlor game at a party and went on from there."

Gordon offered Charles a wry smile. "So you see Amanda may prove useful to you in many ways," he said. "It's possible if you secure the right spirit guide she might even write your book for you as Patience Worth did for Mrs. Curran."

Pat moved to stand at Charles' side and with an admiring smile, she told him, "I'm sure you'd prefer to write your own book, wouldn't you?"

"That is my idea," he said.

"But a book written by a regular author is such a bore," Aunt Clem protested. "Think of the stir it would create if you could produce one dictated by a woman dead for more than a century."

Charles smiled thinly. "You tempt me, Aunt Clem. But mightn't I have some trouble making the public believe that Amanda had dictated the book?"

Anita found the whole conversation increasingly unbelievable. They were talking about Amanda as if she were one of them. As if she still had influence after all her years in the grave. She glanced over at the smug portrait with the hard, cold eyes of the suspected murderess gazing down at them. And once again she experienced feelings of despair and frustration, as if a clammy hand from the grave had reached out and touched her, as if she'd been warned that in the ancient corridors of Shorecliff unknown dangers lurked for her and the husband she loved.

Gordon broke into her reverie by saying, "We haven't heard a thing from Anita on the subject. I'm sure she must have some ideas about the kind of book her husband should write."

Conscious that the eyes of all the others had been suddenly focused on her Anita attempted a wan smile. "I want him to write whatever he enjoys doing best," she said quietly.

"Spoken like a devoted wife," Gordon's amusement plainly showed.

Pat raised her eyebrows. "But is she being helpful? She's certainly not offering Charles any concrete suggestion!"

Anita had become slowly aware of Pat's catering to Charles. Pat had moved across the room to stand next to him, and her almost continual admiring glances must have been noticed by the others. Now she was taking it on herself to defend him when no defense was necessary. It seemed pretty clear that Pat was doing all she could to win Charles' good will. Maybe even more than that.

Anita smiled across at the other girl with an assurance that she did not feel. "I prefer to allow Charles a free rein."

Gordon's mocking smile was for her. "But surely you must sometimes find that dangerous?"

She knew what he meant but she wasn't going to be tripped up by him. "No," she said firmly, "I think it's worth the risk."

Aunt Clem rose from her chair and smoothed her drab black dress. "I find our conversation becoming boring," she said. "And I'm dreadfully tired. It's time for us to return to our own side of the house."

Goodnights were said and Aunt Clem invited Anita for tea the following afternoon. Gordon held her hand just a little longer than necessary and urged that she visit his shop after she'd settled down.

Pat closed the door after them and came back to Anita and Charles with what appeared to be a suspiciously relieved smile. "Have a last drink with me?" she suggested.

"A very short one," Charles told her.

"I'll just take a little ginger ale," Anita told Pat as she moved to the sideboard.

Charles again went over to study Amanda's portrait with narrowed eyes. Anita was puzzled by his fixation. He had made no reference to Amanda or her history before coming to Shorecliff.

Pat returned with their drinks and faced them with a smile.

"I expect Anita found Aunt Clem a trifle overwhelming."

Charles laughed. "I'd forgotten how formidable she can be."

"Is she always so strong in her opinions?" Anita asked.

Pat rolled her eyes. "She was on her best behavior tonight. Wait until you know her better."

"I'm not sure I want to," Anita protested, sipping her drink.

"The one I feel sorry for is Gordon." Pat's pretty face clouded slightly. "He's a kind, intelligent young man and he's devoted his life to Clem with very little thanks for it."

Charles nodded. "He seems to have gotten rather bitter."

"Wouldn't you, in his place?" Pat wanted to know. "I'm sure Gordon would have married long ago if it wasn't for his mother."

Anita said, "She mentioned something about him being a business failure. Yet he seems very dedicated to his antique shop."

"He did have some financial difficulties," the other girl admitted with a sigh. "I believe he invested rather heavily in some older paintings and later had to sacrifice them since there was no market for them here. And then Clem is always crying poor mouth and blaming everyone else. Yet she never earned a penny in her life."

"I suppose she was also looking for some of Aunt Clare's money," Charles suggested. "Since it originally came from her brother, she'd regard it as family money."

Pat smiled bitterly. "She made the mistake of giving Clare too many hints on that very subject. All that she left her in the will were a half-dozen good Wedgwood pieces."

"Surely Gordon could break the ties and leave here if he liked," Anita said.

"I suppose he could," Pat agreed. "But he's easy-going. He likes the local scene and gets great pleasure from operating the antique shop. I'm afraid he'll never move while his mother is alive. After that it's liable to be too late." She gave Charles another admiring glance. "He lacks Charles' aggressiveness. According to the stories of their boyhood, he always did."

Anita was again annoyed by Pat's unabashed flattery of her husband. She held up her empty glass. "Time for bed," she told him.

Pat saw them to the bottom of the stairway. "I'm sure you'll find your bedroom comfortable," she said. "The sun comes in there nicely in the morning. You can come down any time you like for breakfast. Mrs. Miller is good about that."

Anita was filled with a conflict of emotions as she mounted the broad stairway with Charles. Certainly it was pleasant to realize they were the owners of such a fine old mansion. But there were restrictions that spoiled the legacy — like living in the same house with the young, attractive Pat. And that chic female had apparently decided she must charm Charles. It was awkward.

And there was also the problem of the adjoining house. It made Aunt Clem and her son next door neighbors. She liked Gordon but she was positive his mother would be difficult to keep on a friendly basis. To top everything else there was Charles' strange behavior since arriving at Shorecliff. As they walked down the shadowed corridor to their room she glanced at him and was troubled by his set, weary expression.

In the privacy of the bedroom she said, "I'm not sure it's going to work out, Charles. I think we should talk it all over before we do any unpacking."

He had his jacket off and stood staring at her. "What do you mean?"

"It's going to be difficult to fit in here," she said.

"Not for me."

"You're already showing the strain," she told him. "Even though you may not want to admit it." She gazed around the richly furnished bedroom with its period pieces and heavy yellow drapes. "I feel this is not a happy house. And if we remain here some of the unhappiness may taint us."

He halted in the unbuttoning of his shirt. "But that's pure nonsense!" he protested.

"Is it?" she said. "Pat has admitted she's disappointed the house wasn't left to her. Aunt Clem also feels we did her out of money. I suppose Gordon doesn't care but he's bitter and twisted from the life he's led." She paused before making her most important point. "And then there's this strange obsession you've suddenly acquired about Amanda."

Charles frowned. "What about it?"

"I don't think it's healthy," she said. "I'm not sure you're sufficiently over your accident to stand the stress of living down here. You complained of a bad headache this afternoon."

He moved away to hang his jacket in the closet. When he came back he glared at her and said, "Are you questioning my mental state?"

"No," she said, shocked by the coldness of his tone. "But all this talk of ghosts and old murders frightens me."

"All old houses have stories attached to

them. Many of them sinister."

"Amanda's story surely is," she blurted out. "I can't bear to look at that portrait. Her expression is so smug! And those eyes! They are the eyes of a person capable of murder!"

Charles' face was grim. "Why do you choose to accuse her? You have no grounds."

"She was that sort of person! The account of how she became so pious and then had her face actually preserved in a porcelain mask makes it clear she was a strange person. I find the idea of that mask horrible! She was never able to smile again!"

"But she did preserve her beauty unblemished."

"In a kind of death mask!" Anita said. "I find it all macabre. And I don't know why you want to delve in the past and do her story."

"I believe it would make a fine novel," Charles said quietly.

Tears brimmed in Anita's eyes. "And I'm terrified that this old house has done something to you. Since you've seen that portrait of Amanda you've been under some kind of evil spell. It's as if she's bewitched you!"

Charles seemed touched by her sudden tears. He came forward quickly and took her in his arms. "You mustn't let such foolish thoughts upset you," he said. "I was proud of you tonight. Especially when you told them you wanted me to write whatever would make me happy."

She looked up at him. Her eyes were moist. "I'm not nearly as pretty as Pat," she said.

"But you're much more beautiful to me," he told her gently and pressed his lips to hers for a long kiss.

In a way she was placated. Some of her fears were allayed. But she lay awake beside him long after he'd gone to sleep. She tried to think it all out as she gazed into the darkness and she only became more confused. Again and again that horror returned to her, that frightening few seconds when she'd experienced the sensation of a shadow passing between her and Charles. And afterwards there had been the overwhelming scent of Attar of Roses.

At last sleep came to her. But it was a light, restless sleep and she soon awakened from it with a start. Sitting up in bed she was at once aware that Charles was no longer beside her. A small gasp escaped her lips and she groped for her dressing gown, flung it over her shoulders and stumbled across the darkened room. She found the hall door and opened it and went hurrying along the corridor towards the stairs. The corridor was unlighted but there was a dim glow from the stairway where a night light was apparently left on.

When she was a short distance from the stairs she caught a glimpse of Charles descending them. He was almost a third of the way down. She realized it must have been his rising that had awakened her. He seemed to be in a dazed, sleepwalking state. She had come very close to the head of the stairs when a weird figure appeared out of the shadows.

And it came straight toward her with claw-like hands outstretched!

CHAPTER THREE

Anita's lips were sealed by the terror that came over her. As the figure emerged from the shadows she recognized its pale, shining oval of a face as a replica of Amanda's in the painting downstairs. The figure was clothed in voluminous black in the fashion of another day and a dark shawl was draped over her head and shoulders. Now the frightening claw-like hands were poised above a crouching Anita. There was something that looked like a giant hat pin in one of them.

Stumbling backward, Anita was still unable to dodge the poised weapon. She felt a sharp sting of pain as it descended in the region of her arm. Then she finally let out a tortured cry as the aroma of Attar of Roses swirled about and nearly suffocated her.

Right after that she fainted.

When she came to she was in the big bed again. Charles, Pat and a third person, all looking grave, stood at the bedside.

The gray-haired stranger with the serious, lined face, asked, "How do you feel?"

She touched her tongue to her dry lips. "What happened?"

"That's what we'd like to know," the grave-faced man said. "Your husband found you collapsed at the head of the stairs."

She frowned in swift recollection. "I know, now," she said. "I was following him when an apparition came at me out of the shadows." She glanced from the stranger to Charles. "It was Amanda!"

Charles and the stranger exchanged significant looks. Then Charles leaned over the bed and said, "This is Dr. Wilson. I've been telling him that you were upset and nervous earlier in the night. He isn't sure what happened to you. You had some kind of mild convulsion. It was frightening."

"But I've told you," she said, staring at him. "Amanda's ghost attacked me. She had a giant hat pin in her hand. She plunged it into me and there was a sickening smell of roses."

Dr. Wilson studied her with a strange expression. "I'd be inclined to say you dreamed most of that, Mrs. Shore. You were aroused from sleep in the middle of the night. Then in the excitement you were taken with this seizure."

"But I saw the pale china face. It was horrible!"

"You experienced some delirium and these fantasies were based on the conversation you had earlier in the evening," the doctor said quietly. "Have you ever had an attack like this before?"

"It was Amanda's ghost!" she insisted. "That is why I fainted."

Dr. Wilson's face showed concern. "I'm afraid you don't realize what happened to you," he told her. "You have been unconscious for several hours. And you showed definite signs of convulsion at the beginning. Is there any history of epilepsy in your family?"

Outraged, Anita sat up part way and stormed, "Why won't you listen to me!"

The doctor took her by the shoulders and pressed her gently back on the pillow. "Please don't upset yourself unduly, Mrs. Shore. I'm only trying to help you."

"There's nothing wrong with my health," Anita insisted. "I missed Charles from the bed and went out into the hall after him. Along the way I was intercepted by the apparition."

The doctor sighed. "We won't argue the

60

point now, Mrs. Shore. You seem to have made a satisfactory recovery so we needn't worry too much. But do take it easy during the day and when you're feeling better have your husband bring you to my office in the village for a thorough examination. I'd like to try and discover what may have caused your illness and prevent another spell."

"Very well, Doctor," she said wearily. "What time is it?"

"Dawn," he said. "It's a few minutes after six. I've left a mild sedative with your husband. Take a dose of it and get some more sleep."

With that he nodded to her and left with Pat. When she and Charles were alone she looked up at her husband with troubled eyes.

"You were the cause of what happened," she accused him. "Why did you get up in the middle of the night and go downstairs?"

Charles, in dressing gown and pajamas, looked sheepish. "It's hard to explain. I woke up and couldn't get to sleep. I began thinking of the possibilities of doing Amanda's story and I kept thinking of the portrait. I decided to go downstairs and have a cigarette and look around the living room. I felt that after ten or fifteen minutes down there I might be able to settle back to sleep again."

Anita's blue eyes opened wide. "She worked some spell on you! It was Amanda who forced you to go down there! Her evil spirit is still alive in this house and she sees you as a new conquest!"

"You're talking wildly!"

"Perhaps," she said, rising on an elbow in her excitement. "But she was there at the head of the stairs waiting to halt me. She was not going to let me interfere between her and you."

"You've been ill," her husband remonstrated. "I don't want to argue this with you."

"You'll never change my mind nor will the doctor," she said, and then a pleading expression coming to her pretty face, she begged, "Let's leave here in the morning before anything else awful happens."

He sat on the bed and took her hands in his. "What else can happen?"

"She'll go on trying to kill me and capture you with her witchery," Anita warned him tensely. "She means to own you."

"I have the medicine the doctor left," he said. "I'll give you some. You'll get more rest and feel differently."

"No sedative will change my mind about what is going on here," she warned him.

But she did take the medicine and shortly after fell into a deep sleep. When she woke up the sun was streaming in through the bedroom window as Pat had promised. It was late morning and she got up and went into the attached bathroom and washed. She was dizzy from the sedative and not until she'd rinsed her face in very cold water did her head begin to clear. She had slipped on her dressing gown and was in the bedroom, just about to select her clothes for the day when the door from the hallway opened and Charles appeared carrying a tray.

Seeing her standing in the middle of the room his face brightened. "I didn't know you were awake. But I brought up breakfast anyway."

She smiled at him. "You must have started the day early!"

"Only an hour or so ago to be honest," he said. "You sit in the easy chair and I'll bring the small table up beside it for your tray."

Anita enjoyed the attention he was giving her. She sat by the window and let him put down the tray and arrange it for her. The breakfast was too generous and she just took the juice, cereal and toast and a single boiled egg, skipping bacon and a second egg. As she took her coffee she sat back and stared at her husband with gentle eyes.

"Sometimes you surprise me with your consideration."

He smiled. "Admit it's a rare occasion when I do."

"I won't say that," she promised him. "Not publicly at any rate."

He stood watching her. "You're looking much better."

"I'm feeling it," she insisted. Looking up at him demurely, she asked, "Well, have you decided what we'll do?"

"Do about what?"

"Stay on here or not," she said.

He shrugged. "Of course we'll stay on here. We'll both feel better when we've managed another night's rest."

"I wish I was as sure of that as you seem to be, Charles," she said soberly.

He frowned. "But you're being ridiculous. You haven't given the place a chance. Pat likes you and wants you to stay."

"Why are you so sure?"

Charles' handsome face showed embarrassment. "She told me so. She says she has looked forward to our coming."

Her eyes met his. "Looked forward to your coming is what she means. Oh, Charles, can't you see it? This girl is interested in you!"

He shook his head. "First it's a ghost who's trying to influence me and now you say it's Pat! What's happened to you, darling?"

She gave him a pitying look. "You want this trouble," she said. "You're really anxious for it. So anxious you just won't listen to me at all. I can't reach you anymore and we've only been at Shorecliff less than twenty-four hours."

Charles sighed and looked down at his feet. "It's too bad you had this spell just when we got here. It's upset you and I can understand it. But Dr. Wilson will check you and fix you up."

"I don't need a doctor," she said. "I know what happened. That ghost stabbed me with something last night. My arm even feels sore." She opened her dressing gown and inspected the upper part of her left arm. Just above the elbow there was a small black and blue spot. "You see," she said triumphantly.

Charles looked worried. "Probably happened when you fell."

She slipped her dressing gown on again

and stared at him incredulously. "You don't believe any of it, do you?"

"Let's not argue about it," he said.

"All right, I won't discuss it anymore. I'll only say what I said before, we should get away while we can."

He spread his hands in despair. "We've had this lovely old house left to us, plenty of money to operate it and I've had the seed of a great novel handed to me. What more could we ask for?"

"To be back in our apartment and safe in our love again," she told him quietly.

This seemed to touch him. He knelt by her chair. "Darling, nothing can ever come between us. You know that."

She shook her head sadly. "There are things working against us in this house that neither of us understand. Forces beyond any human control. If we defy them we are bound to be confused and suffer." But she knew, even as he sealed her warning with a kiss, that he was not listening to her. He was already lost in his dream of recreating the world of the heartless Amanda.

It was noon when she went downstairs. Even after the ordeal of the night she was feeling almost herself again. The extra sleep had done her good and despite the apprehensions that wracked her she was prepared to begin this new life at Shorecliff. Since Charles wanted to remain she was left with no choice.

She had put on a smartly-styled short sleeved yellow dress and she was glad she'd picked it because Pat was her usual chic self in a split skirt of blue and a white blouse with a low neckline. She was standing in the doorway of the living room when Anita came down.

"Good to see you back on your feet," Pat said.

"I'm rarely ill," Anita told her.

"So Charles says," Pat said with a friendly air. "You've just had breakfast so I don't suppose you'll want anything more to eat just now."

"No."

"I should show you around," Pat said hesitantly. "But that had better wait for another day. Why don't you come out and sit in the conservatory. It's really no more than an overgrown bay window but we dignify it with the title and it's really quite pleasant. We have screens permanently installed so there is lots of air on these summer days. And because of the glass overhead it's warmer than outdoors."

"Sounds pleasant," she smiled.

Pat led her along a narrow passage-way that ended in the glassed-in area. It was filled with enormous potted plants and the sun poured in to make it a relaxing spot. Wicker chairs and a coffee table comprised the furnishings.

Pat indicated the surroundings with a gesture. "Each section of the house has one of these. Aunt Clem has only a few plants in hers. But Clare had a green thumb and so we've done better. It's pleasant here even on wet days."

"I imagine it would be," Anita said as she sat down. She looked out the wide expanse of windows and saw there were no other houses in sight. Just a barrier of evergreens surrounding the flat lawns and the cliff on the ocean side of the old mansion. "Do you find it lonely in winter?"

Pat nodded. She was seated opposite her and had taken up a bit of embroidery and automatically began to work at it as she talked. "When the winds begin to howl and the snow drifts several feet high one does feel isolated. Aunt Clem has solved the problem by going off to Florida for January, February and March."

Anita raised her eyebrows. "Does Gordon go with her?"

"Of course," Pat said with a humorous

look on her pretty face. "Don't think his mother would leave him here alone at the mercy of us village girls!"

"Worse things could happen to him," Anita said quietly.

"Thank you," Pat said and went on working at her embroidery. Nothing was said for several minutes. A fly buzzed lazily in the hot sun, from outside came the pleasant chirping of birds; the smell of sweet hay permeated the air and invaded the screens of the conservatory. It was all so deceptively peaceful, Anita thought.

She said, "This is a wonderful location for a house."

"I'm glad you like it," Pat said politely. And with her eyes on her work, she added, "After last night I was afraid you mightn't stay."

"It is our home now."

Pat lifted her eyes from the embroidery to meet hers. "It's good you feel that way. I'm sure this place means a great deal to Charles."

Yes, Anita thought, you want him to stay. You want him to stay badly enough so you'll even put up with me. Aloud she said, "He does seem entranced with it here."

"I haven't any idea what happened last night," Pat went on awkwardly. "But I'm certain it's not likely to happen again."

Anita's interest was caught. "Why do you say that?" She began to wonder if the girl opposite her might have had the inspiration to play the role of Amanda's ghost the previous night. It was really much more likely than encountering a true apparition.

Pat was embarrassed. "I mean you haven't been ill often. It was probably the excitement and strain."

Anita eyed her solemnly. "You know that I believe I saw Amanda's ghost?"

"The doctor said that was a kind of delirium."

"But it wasn't," she told her firmly.

Pat dropped her eyes to her embroidery once more and her fingers worked nimbly. "I see," she said quietly.

"You claimed that Aunt Clare saw the ghost more than once," she went on.

"Aunt Clare was terribly old and given to imaginings. And then that Mary Vane exerted a dreadful influence over her."

"But odd things have happened here."

"Nothing that should bother you."

"I am bothered now by my husband's strange fascination with Amanda's history. I would rather he work on some other story. And I don't believe he ever thought of that murderess until he returned to Shorecliff."

"I think you're worrying about that too much," Pat commented.

Summing up the girl's attitude Anita began to be even more convinced that Pat might have decided to eliminate her by assuming the role of the phantom murderess. Pat was obviously attracted to Charles and believed that they had taken the estate from her. What easier solution than to rid herself of Charles' wife, marry him and get both a handsome husband and the estate. Anita would do well to be wary of Aunt Clare's adopted daughter.

She said, "You seem to be on Charles' side."

Pat smiled faintly. "Let's say I'm in a position to be more objective than you. Are you still planning to have tea this afternoon with Aunt Clem?"

Anita considered. "Yes. I think so."

"You needn't if you're not feeling up to it. I can give her a message telling her you've been ill."

"No, I think I might as well face it," Anita said wryly. "Is there any direct connection between the two houses?"

"No doors or anything like that," Pat told her. "Not even the cellars are joined."

"Then you have to actually go outside to get to the other house?"

Pat nodded. "It is a completely separate house except for the common wall. The brothers who built Shorecliff wanted to live side by side but they had some rather strong ideas about privacy."

"It's understandable," she said. "Are you joining me for tea at Aunt Clem's?"

Pat smiled. "No. I told her last night I had to take the station wagon into the village for some repairs."

Anita thought this was just an excuse, that Pat wouldn't have gone to the tea party anyway. She said, "You don't exactly yearn for Aunt Clem's company."

"Not exactly," Pat said dryly. "I've lived here far too long."

"But surely you must find Gordon likable."

Pat paused in her embroidery. "I do."

Anita proceeded cautiously with her next question, "I wonder a romance hasn't sprung up between you two."

Pat blushed. She said, "With his mother here as a watchdog?"

Anita smiled. "Doesn't love laugh at locksmiths?"

"And there's a rare locksmith," Pat said grimly. "She has her talons a quarter-inch deep in Gordon's hide."

"He doesn't seem mother-dominated in spite of his deference to her."

"He is and he isn't," Pat said, looking at her. "I may as well tell you the truth. You're smart enough to guess it anyway. Gordon and I dated for a while in a furtive, nervous sort of way." She sighed. "It wasn't much fun."

"I'm sorry," Anita said. "I think he needs someone."

"So do I," Pat admitted freely. "But not Gordon. He's nice and kind and has so many good things about him. But it didn't work out. I guess we can blame it on old rabbit-teeth. Her menace hovered over us."

"Rabbit-teeth?"

"I mean Aunt Clem," Pat said. "You've surely noticed that mouth of hers."

Anita was forced to smile. "I have. So you and Gordon don't date anymore?"

"Not really. Oh, once in awhile we may go to a movie or one of the summer play-houses together. But weeks go by and we hardly see each other."

Anita was a victim of mixed emotions. She appreciated Pat's apparent honesty and lack of reticence in discussing herself. Yet she wondered if this wasn't a pose to dispel any suspicions concerning her. She felt Pat was being too carelessly frank and there was more to the story than she was telling. On the surface it seemed that she was much more drawn to Charles than Gordon. And because she had this crush on Charles it was up to her to be especially wary.

Pat put down her embroidery and rose suddenly. "I've got to speak to Mrs. Miller about dinner tonight," she said. "Will you excuse me?"

"Of course."

Anita sat there for some minutes after Pat left her. And then she began to get uneasy. She wondered where Charles might be and decided to try and find him. She realized that Pat had been careful to make no mention of him.

Retracing her way down the passage she arrived back in the main hallway. She glanced into the living room but it was deserted. For a moment her eyes dwelt on that portrait that had weirdly come to play such a part in her life. Even at this distance Amanda's eyes seemed to bite into her.

Going back to the hall she encountered Mrs. Miller. She was a thin, wiry woman with the weathered face of one who has lived her life in the country. And there was something else about her, a furtive sullenness that left Anita wondering.

Anita asked her, "Have you seen Mr. Shore?"

The dour woman said, "He was in the library."

"Thank you," she said. "That's just down the hall, isn't it?"

"Second door on the left," Mrs. Miller said without any trace of friendliness and went on up the stairs.

Anita made her way down to the second door on the left as Mrs. Miller had suggested. She found it almost closed. Hesitantly pushing it open she was startled to see Charles seated in a chair behind the room's single large desk with Pat at his side, her shapely hand resting on his shoulder. They were both so intent on a book he held open on the desk that neither noticed her entrance.

She took a step inside and cleared her throat. "Here you are!"

Pat looked startled and quickly withdrew her hand from Charles' shoulder. But Anita found her husband not at all upset. He gave her a casual glance and said, "I'm reading a family history. It's handwritten. Set down by my grandfather. It's tremendously helpful."

"I'm sure it must be," Anita said with a

knowing smile. "Did Pat find it for you?"

Pat remained completely poised. "As a matter of fact, I did," she said. "And I stopped by now to find out how he liked it."

"How helpful you are," Anita said.

Pat smiled obliquely. "You'll both excuse me," she said. And she hurried out of the room, going past Anita without glancing at her again.

Charles remained intent on the ancient manuscript. Anita advanced across the room to stand where Pat had been and study the crabbed writing of the hand-written book over his shoulder.

She said, "What have you learned about Amanda?"

He raised his eyes to her with mild surprise. "Not as much as I'd have liked," he said. "From my grandfather's comments I judge that he believed she did kill that young sea captain."

"He came to this house and was never seen to leave it."

"Not evidence enough," Charles mused. "It would have been dark before he left. He wouldn't have to be seen."

She smiled at him ruefully. "You don't want to accept her as a murderess."

"I'll write her story either way," he said.

"I'd like to be sure before I begin."

"She'll be satisfied just as long as you make her live again," Anita murmured sadly.

He frowned. "What's that?"

"It's not important," she told him. "I'm going upstairs to unpack a few of our things. Then I'm going next door for tea later."

His eyes were on the book again. "With Aunt Clem?" he inquired absently.

"Yes." But she knew he was no longer listening so she went on out and back upstairs.

One of the first things she took out of the boxes was a framed double study of Charles and herself. It had been taken by a photographer friend and showed them with heads together smiling against a background of Boston Common. She'd always kept it on her bedroom dresser.

And because it was a precious reminder of their good days she felt it important to put it on the dresser here. Perhaps it would be a lucky omen to dispel the evil spirit of Amanda which she felt could threaten their marriage.

She carefully placed the framed photo prominently on the dresser and then went back to some other unpacking. She

77

stopped at three and rested for a half-hour before getting ready for tea with Aunt Clem at four. Pat had probably left for the village ages ago, she decided, since the house was silent and seemingly deserted. Charles would be in the library and the servants in the rear section of the old house.

At four o'clock she went down to pay her visit to Aunt Clem, neat in a dark blue afternoon dress. The door of the other house was an exact duplicate of their own and it was opened by a tiny little woman with white hair.

She smiled at Anita, "Mrs. Morehouse is expecting you," she said. "Go right on in to the parlor."

Anita thanked her and headed for the living room. Aunt Clem, in her usual black dress, was seated there with another woman. The other woman was striking. Her hair was jet-black and she had an olive complexion and a strong face with deep-set, shadowed eyes. There was a hint of beauty in her gaunt features, as well as the suggestion of power. Her eyebrows were too heavy for best effect and the drab gray dress she wore did little to enhance her mannish figure.

Aunt Clem came forward with a smile

on her rabbit-face. "I have a surprise for you, my dear. This is my guest, Mary Vane."

"Mary Vane!" Anita gasped. "The spiritualist?"

"I am the same Mary Vane," the dark woman acknowledged with a stony smile. "It seems my fame has spread more widely than I thought."

Aunt Clem turned to her. "But we were discussing you next door. Last night at the welcoming party for Anita and Charles." The pinched, white face took on a faintly roguish expression as she confided to Anita, "The truth is that Mary was here as my guest even then."

"But you didn't mention it!" Anita said.

The old woman chuckled. "I enjoy my little secrets, my dear. I've had Miss Vane here for several days. I wouldn't want this to go any further but I've been trying to get in touch with Clare's spirit. There are some things I think she should explain to me."

"I see."

"I didn't want Patricia to know," Aunt Clem went on. "At least not until Miss Vane and I had been able to hold several seances. It doesn't matter now."

Anita asked, "Were you able to reach Aunt Clare?"

Mary Vane replied in her deep, authoritative voice, "We contacted her spirit. But she is very troubled. She was not able to talk to us coherently."

"Poor dear!" said Aunt Clem with a sigh. "I think she regrets some of her hasty decisions." And then she quickly changed the subject. "But we mustn't dwell on that. We have you here to be entertained. Do sit down, Anita."

The little old woman with the white hair darted in to serve tea. She did so unobtrusively and with a deft skill born of years in service. Aunt Clem babbled on about the seances and how Miss Vane had caused a table to rise in the air several inches, and the intricate spirit rappings that had manifested themselves and the guide, Elsie, who served as Miss Vane's contact with the great beyond.

"Elsie is the spirit of a little girl drowned in the bay here nearly fifty years ago," Aunt Clem twittered. "Miss Vane and I searched out her gravestone in the Pennbridge cemetery."

"How interesting," Anita said politely, although her thoughts were racing on other subjects. So Mary Vane, the medium, had actually been in this other part of the house last night. She had been there when the spirit of Amanda had materialized. Could the medium have played any part in that even though she was in this section of the twin buildings and there were no connecting doors between them? It seemed likely there could be a link to the happening since ghosts had the power to penetrate walls at will.

She told the medium, "My husband will be delighted to know that you are here. He has been talking of trying to contact you."

Mary Vane's heavy eyebrows lifted. "Really?"

"Yes," Anita went on. "He is interested in doing a book on Amanda Shore. And as part of his research he is anxious to try and reach her in a seance."

The dark woman nodded. "The murderess, or purported to be. I remember. Very interesting."

"When I go back I'll tell him you're here," Anita said. "You're not planning to leave."

Aunt Clem spoke up in her high-pitched voice. "We won't allow that. She must remain until some of the veils have been penetrated."

"I shall certainly stay a few more days," Mary Vane said in her deep, odd voice that seemed to echo hollowly under ordinary conditions. "I shall look forward to a talk with your husband."

Anita remained a while longer and then went back to her own part of the house. She went directly to the library to find Charles but he wasn't there. From the library window she saw the station wagon parked outside. Pat must have returned as well. She wondered if she and Charles were together.

With a sinking feeling she decided it was useless to try and counter every move Pat made. And she went upstairs to the bedroom. As soon as she opened the door the scent of Attar of Roses assailed her nostrils. And she suddenly noted something awry on the dresser. With an angry gasp she rushed across the room to examine the damage. It was the photo of her and Charles.

The glass had been smashed and the photos ripped from the frame!

CHAPTER FOUR

Anita stared at the vandalized frame with shock and horror. Placing the damaged photo on the dresser she looked around the big bedroom with fear in her eyes. There was no other sign of an intruder.

And yet someone had come into the room and destroyed the photo of herself and Charles in the short while she'd been next door. It had to be either the evil spirit of Amanda or the work of some living person who had taken this way of venting his hatred of her.

Pat?

It was a possibility. She was positive that beneath her calm exterior there was a seething inferno of temperament. Given strong enough motives she had an idea Pat would be capable of anything. And what stronger motives were there than love and money? Pat would win both if she could take Charles from her. So it might very well be Pat who was doing the mischief in an effort to upset her and eventually make her run away from Shorecliff and Charles. The Attar of Roses need not have wafted from another world, but could have been carefully sprayed about at the time of each attack to confuse her.

Yet the notion that she was battling a real ghost continued to linger in her mind. And one thing that strengthened this belief was the change in Charles. In the short period they'd been in the old mansion a barrier had come between them. And she feared the wall of dissension might become wider. Charles suddenly seemed to have succumbed to the spell of the family home and to be especially obsessed with the long dead Amanda.

It was Amanda whom she feared more than anyone else, because she believed the evil spirit of that other-century beauty still dominated Shorecliff in some eerie fashion. She had sensed it on that first afternoon of her arrival and her apprehensions continued to grow.

Her impulse now was to face Charles and insist that they leave before anything worse happened. But she knew he wouldn't listen to her, just as he wouldn't properly try to understand what had happened in the night; that the supposed convulsion she'd had was not the result of any strain or illness on her part. It had been induced in some way by the phantom figure that had attacked her. She clearly recalled the poised hat pin and the jab of pain it had left in her arm. But Charles had calmly accepted the bruise she'd suffered as the result of the fall when she'd collapsed.

Considering all this there could not be much hope of reasoning with her handsome husband. In fact it was very likely he would become more determined to stay on in the mansion when he learned that Mary Vane was a guest next door. This opened a new avenue of fear in her thoughts. She felt that the spiritualist was a strange type and perhaps completely unscrupulous in the ways she used her powers to communicate with the world of the dead.

With all her diabolical skill Mary Vane might easily impress Charles and bring him to a point of more confusion. He would certainly ask her to help him contact the spirit of Amanda Shore. What would take place after that she hardly dared guess.

Slowly she prepared for dinner. She hadn't a doubt that Mary Vane would be over and it would be a time of crisis. She was standing before the dresser mirror when Charles opened the door.

Studying his reflection in the mirror she could see that he looked weary and preoccupied. She turned around to greet him, saying, "I thought you might soon be up."

"I've been busy with that history," he said. "I just finished it."

"I didn't see you in the library when I came in from Aunt Clem's."

He gave her an uneasy glance. "That must have been when I went out back for a few minutes. Pat wanted me to hear the engine of the station wagon. It has been giving her trouble."

Anita restrained the anger she felt. She might have known. She said, "I've been having some trouble of my own."

He further annoyed her by standing there rather moodily and saying, "If there were just some more sources of information."

She frowned. "Information about what?"

"Amanda and her family," he said, not taking heed of her annoyance in his preoccupied state. "My grandfather largely skipped over her story."

"He was probably wise," she said.

Charles stared at her. "Why do you say that?"

"Wasn't she notorious? A reputed murderess! Why should he dwell on the dark side of the family in putting down his history?"

"I think Amanda has been unfairly dealt with," Charles objected. "No one was ever able to prove she killed that young captain. In fact I consider it highly unlikely." His tone was growing more strained.

Anita took a step toward him. "That's because you're under her spell now!"

"Don't say such things!"

"I mean it," Anita protested. "She wants to claim you. To have you defend her. I can feel her malice everywhere in this house!"

Her husband's handsome face registered concern. "Can you actually be jealous of a girl dead for so many years?"

She shook her head. "You have it wrong. It is she who is jealous of me. And she's proven it again."

"What are you talking about?"

Anita moved back to the dresser and picked up the damaged photo and took it over to him. She said, "What do you make of that? The glass broken and the photo ripped from the frame?"

He studied it with a furrowed brow. Then he raised his eyes to meet hers. "Why connect this with Amanda?"

"I left it on the dresser when I went to Aunt Clem's. It was in perfect condition. When I returned it was like this and the air around the dresser was reeking with Attar of Roses — Amanda's perfume!"

He eyed her dubiously. "Are you sure you're feeling well?"

"That's insulting!" she declared in anger. "You're treating me as if I weren't mentally alert. You behaved the same way when the doctor was here!"

"You did have that convulsion," he reminded her.

"Because of something that phantom did to me," she replied. "I felt the jab of a needle in my arm. But you don't believe that!"

Charles shrugged, the photo still in his hand. "Dr. Wilson blamed your fantasy on the convulsion and blackout."

"It's no fantasy!"

He moved by her to the dresser. After standing there a moment he looked her way. "I can't smell any of this rose perfume you've been raving about."

She crossed over to him, frustrated with rage. "It's been some time since I found the photo this way. The perfume has dissipated!"

He said nothing for a moment. Then in

a reproving tone he told her, "You don't have to play a trick like this to get away from here!"

Her eyebrows lifted. "What do you mean?"

"I've been talking it over with Pat," he said. "And she agrees that it doesn't seem to be good for you here. Perhaps you should go back to the city. We could do with a small apartment in Boston. And we can afford an extra place now. It might be better to get one furnished."

Anita could scarcely credit what she heard but she somehow maintained a calm front. "Did Pat give you all this good advice?"

"She pointed out that Shorecliff seems bad for your nerves. You did have that spell. And an apartment in town will come in handy. I'll be using some of the Boston libraries and museums for research. It means I'll be making frequent visits there."

"Your idea is that I should maintain the apartment there while you live down here for the major part of the time?"

"Not a major part," he objected. "But at least until I get a good start with my book."

Her pretty face looked bitter. "I might be able to hold my own against Amanda," she said acidly. "But when she and Pat work together against me I'm not so sure."

"What kind of craziness is this?" he demanded, placing the broken frame on the dresser.

"I'm just telling you how convenient your arrangement would be for you and Pat."

"That's a miserable slur on Pat," he told her. "And she doesn't deserve it!"

"I'm sure she doesn't," Anita snapped back. "She's just as pure and unsullied in thought and deed as your precious Amanda."

His face was dark and contorted with rage. "You're jealous," he said. "Jealous that I'm finally going to write my book!"

It was too much. She half-sobbed, "I've always wanted you to do a book."

"But not this one."

"I hadn't even *heard* of Amanda until we came here. But if you must know I don't think it's the proper kind of subject for you to tackle in your state of mind. You're still only half-well. You had that bad injury. I'm certain these dark moods are all part of it."

He smiled coldly. "It won't do, Anita," he said. "I can see through your game. My guess is this photo's glass was broken during the trip down and when you found

it damaged you ripped out the picture itself and concocted this wild story of a
ghost maliciously doing it."

"Why should I do that?"

"To try to force me to leave here and
drop my book," he said. "I've worked and
waited for this chance too long to be
duped out of it. And when it comes to
questionable mental states, I think the one
under a cloud is you and not me. You had
that spell and now you're trying a mad
stunt like this!"

She faced him firmly. "I won't be frightened away. No matter what!"

"You're changing your tune!" he said
with a contempt she had never seen in him
before.

Not wanting to argue further she turned
and ran out of the bedroom. When she
stepped into the corridor she almost
bumped into Mrs. Miller. At once she suspected that the housekeeper might have
been listening to them.

She said, "Is there something you want?"

Mrs. Miller's weathered face was defiant.
In her sullen way she said, "I came up to
ask if you needed more blankets."

"No. We have a good supply."

"It can be cold at night even at this time
of year," the housekeeper warned.

Anita remained standing by the bedroom door. "I'm certain we'll be all right."

Mrs. Miller gave her a scornful glance. "You know best," she said and she went on down the corridor toward the stairs.

She watched after her and again felt certain the housekeeper had been eavesdropping. But why? It was merely another annoyance in a house that seemed to have more than its share.

Charles came down later and dinner was a stiffly uncomfortable business for all three of them until Pat announced that Mary Vane was staying in the other house. "She's been right next door for three or four days and I didn't know it until I met her and Clem outside this afternoon."

He showed interest at once. "But of course I want to talk with her."

Pat smiled smugly. "I've arranged that. They're all coming over here after dinner." She looked at Anita. "You met Miss Vane at tea this afternoon, didn't you?"

She nodded. "Yes," she said quietly.

"You did?" Charles said with a reproving glance. "Why didn't you mention it to me?"

"I don't believe you gave me a chance to," she said.

"You knew I would be interested," he argued on.

"Well, it can't be all that important," Pat said, taking on the new role of peacemaker. "You'll all be meeting tonight."

Anita saw unhappily that Pat had out-maneuvered her once again. In her upset about discovering the vandalized photograph she had missed telling Charles about the arrival of the medium. And in his present mood, he would at once jump to the conclusion she'd done it deliberately.

At eight sharp the trio from next door arrived. Aunt Clem led Mary Vane in with the air of one bringing them a prize. Gordon lurked in the background with one of his grimly amused smiles. He said little as introductions were made and they all made themselves comfortable in the parlor.

Mary Vane sat in a wing back chair and regarded Charles with her deep-set eyes. "You are interested in the spirit world, Mr. Shore?" she asked in that low, hollow voice.

Charles was standing before the fire-place, facing them all. "I'm interested in a particular member of the spirit world," he said. "Amanda Shore."

Mary Vane's pale face stood out against her dark hair and she smiled thinly. "You are interested in the mystery surrounding her?"

"Yes," he said. And then almost eagerly, "You see I'm using her as the chief figure in a novel I'm projecting. I'm not satisfied with the material on her I've been able to assemble." He paused, then added, "Do you think you could manage to reach her directly?"

The older woman nodded gravely. "It is possible."

"Will you try?"

"When the conditions are proper," she said with no show of emotion. She was wearing the same drab suit she'd worn that afternoon.

"You consider that important?" Charles queried.

"The major factor," Mary Vane avowed. "Elsie, my guide, gets easily mixed up if the channels are not clear."

"How do you know?" Aunt Clem asked.

"I can feel." Mary Vane drew herself up proudly in the chair — an almost beautiful woman with a manner that provoked attention. Anita could see she was impressing Charles a great deal. Just as she'd feared.

"You have success in reaching ghosts of the long dead?" he asked the medium.

"I prefer to use the term apparition," Mary said.

"I see," Charles said deferentially and his

eyes wandered to the portrait of Amanda. "Do you think it possible we could discover the truth about her? Whether or not she really murdered that young captain?"

"More difficult feats have been accomplished."

Gordon Morehouse was standing behind the divan on which his mother and Pat were seated. He glanced across at the opposite side of the room where Anita was standing near the controversial portrait. Gordon's face was quite expressionless but there was a mocking gleam in his eyes.

Pat now spoke up, saying, "Do you think the evil spirit of Amanda might still dominate the house she lived in? That she might still manage to attempt hiding what really happened from us?"

"Anyone familiar with survival after death and visitation between this world and the next would agree that she could," Miss Vane firmly asserted. Her face looked derisive. "I know the attitude of the unbelievers only too well. But mark you, there is no other matter upon which the thoughts and feelings have changed so little since the very earliest times. And though many may claim disbelief in apparitions, in most cases it represents merely a repressed rather than a dispelled primitive emotion.

They waver quickly when something happens to remind them that we know only a small fraction of the secrets of the universe. Recurrences of similar experiences in a particular place or on a particular date can quickly make them fearful. Just as deceiving visions and unexplained sounds may trigger their minds to a superstitious level. Like it or not we all have a healthy reverence for the unknown."

Aunt Clem chirped up. "Miss Vane can do the most marvelous things. At one of our seances she made a table rise from the floor!"

Anita felt she should strike out at the menace of the medium in some way — try to alert her husband to the danger he could face from her. She said, "That floating table business is a popular trick of fake mediums, isn't it?"

Mary Vane's deep-set black eyes fixed on her with a vicious stare. "The true manifestations are often duplicated in a ridiculous fashion by charlatans. But levitations have always been an indication of spirits being present."

"I'm sure Anita meant nothing personal in her statement," Aunt Clem said nervously. She looked to Anita to confirm her words.

Anita decided it might be best to soften what she had said. "I was speaking only in a general way," she said.

"I do not care to be grouped with the average medium," Miss Vane said, her manner suggesting she'd been offended and would not soon forgive Anita.

Charles moved to the center of the room and confronted the medium. "Could we hold a seance here and now?"

Mary Vane hesitated. "I could make the attempt," she said. "I can promise nothing."

"I'd like to try and contact Amanda," Charles went on. "What do you need to begin?"

"A small table," the medium said. "Yet one large enough for us all to group around."

Aunt Clem's pinched, white face lit up. "How exciting!" she said. "Perhaps we may find out about Amanda after all these years."

Gordon said grimly, "Count me out! I'm not up to this kind of space exploration tonight."

His mother glanced at him with annoyance. "You're never agreeable to anything!"

Anita gave Charles a defiant glance. "I'd prefer not to take part either," she said.

"I'm not in a suitable mood. I'd be bound to spoil things."

Mary Vane offered her a sarcastic look. "How kind of you to be truthful. I agree. Unless you feel in sympathy with our quest you should leave the room."

"Gladly," Anita said and turning walked slowly out to the hallway. Behind her she could hear Charles consulting the medium on the proper positioning of the table and how they should all be seated round it. It was another defeat of sorts and maddening to her.

She was no sooner in the front hallway than Gordon joined her. Her husband's cousin studied her from behind his heavy glasses. "I admire your spirit," he said.

"Thanks," she said. "I haven't many camp followers in there."

He gave a disgusted look in the direction of the living room. "I can understand Mother being all taken up by that mumbo-jumbo. She hasn't much else to occupy her mind. But Pat and Charles eating it up is more than I can digest."

Anita sighed. "That Mary Vane is an extremely overpowering personality. She does seem to have some extra dimension or vibration about her. Even her voice is a little scary."

"Part of her stock in trade," Gordon commented lightly. "I'm not saying there aren't any such things as ghosts. But I doubt if they can be reached in Mary Vane's Western Union fashion. I have little faith in her messenger, Elsie. It's my belief that ghosts manifest themselves when and where they want to and not around a medium's table."

She gazed at the young man solemnly. "I agree," she said. "I'm convinced Amanda's evil spirit is hovering about Shorecliff. But I don't think she's going to be managed by any Mary Vane."

"Interesting theory," Gordon agreed. "It's not cold out. Suppose we take a stroll outside while they go ahead with their shenanigans in here?"

"I'd like that," she said.

Darkness had fallen but there were a multitude of stars showing themselves though there was no moon. She could plainly see the outlines of the hedges and the tall trees in the distance and far out on the bay there were the colored lights of buoys and an occasional small craft. In the silence the wash of the waves on the shore could be plainly heard.

They strolled along the gravel walk that

led to the cliff. They'd only gone a few steps when he said, "It's not so good between you and Charles, is it?"

Anita glanced at him in the darkness. "Why do you say that?"

"I could tell by your talk inside. And the way you both behaved. I'm sorry. I don't think you should let this place destroy your happiness."

"Neither do I," she agreed bitterly. "But Charles seems to have different ideas on the matter."

"He could always be stubborn," Gordon said. "We played down here together in the summers years ago. I understand him pretty well."

"This tension between us only began after we arrived," she complained.

"Have you talked to him about living somewhere else?"

"He won't listen," she said. "He's so taken up with that book about Amanda." She paused as their feet crunched in the gravel. "And then there's Pat. She's giving him the wrong kind of encouragement, turning him against me."

"Pat probably thinks she might take your place if you left," Gordon suggested.

"Do you think she'd go that far?"

"Why not? I'm sure she's unhappy about

not being left Shorecliff and getting only a modest amount from the will."

"I'd say Aunt Clare was generous with her," she protested. "After all she was only an adopted daughter. If anyone has a right to complain it would be your mother and you. You were as close to Aunt Clare as Charles. Yet she only left you some Wedgwood pieces."

He laughed lightly. "It was a surprise. But then she felt we were well enough off. And we have our own half of the house."

"That's true," she agreed. And then in an abrupt change she told him, "Pat claims you and she were good friends for a while."

"She did tell you that?" He sounded faintly uneasy.

"Yes," Anita said with mild surprise at his reaction. "It is true, isn't it? You did date her for a time?"

"Sure," he said. "Pat can be quite a girl when she likes. But Mother was always interfering. And with us both living practically in the same house it didn't work out."

"Do you still care for her?"

"I understand her," he said. "I'm not sure I'd like to spend my life with her, although I would like to see her make the right marriage."

101

"She's bound to," Anita said. "She's very attractive."

"I hope she and Charles don't get involved," Gordon said worriedly. "I mean that for both their sakes. I can't see any future for them even if you should accommodatingly step out of the way."

His casual discussion of the possible break-up of her marriage made her feel sick and alone. She wanted to protest but knew she shouldn't. After all he was merely discussing what was only too likely a possibility.

In a tight voice, she said, "I have no idea of stepping aside for them."

"Good girl," he said warmly. "I like a fighter. And a good marriage is worth fighting for." They had come to the edge of the cliff now and the pounding of the waves below was much louder.

Anita shivered slightly and glanced back at Shorecliff. There were lights showing only in the upper windows of their side of the old house. "The seance must be under way. They've turned out all the downstairs lights."

"So they have," he said, following her glance. "In that case the devious Amanda is being summoned at this moment. Don't you fancy you can picture her with that enamel face? The pink cheeks forever set and never brightened by a smile. Just the endless monotony of an expression frozen in porcelain."

"Please!" she begged him. The face of the phantom who had stalked her on the landing was only too vividly recreated by his words.

"I'm sorry," he said sincerely. "I was only joking."

She turned to him. "I don't think Amanda is a subject for jokes. I think of her as a sinister influence."

"You may be right," he admitted. And he stared toward the dark old mansion. "I wonder what they'll find out."

"My guess is they won't find anything," she said. "I think Mary Vane is simply leading Charles on in the hope of getting money out of him."

"It could very well be," Gordon admitted.

"What am I going to do?" she asked brokenly. "He won't leave and he won't give up this book about Amanda!"

Gordon didn't reply for a moment. Then he said, "You'll have to be patient, Anita. I know it's not easy but it's your best hope of winning out."

"Thanks," she said. "It's made all the

difference just having you to talk to."

Again he surprised her by taking her in his arms rather than replying. He kissed her lightly and let her go. Only then did he say, "I'm glad you consider me a friend. And I shouldn't have done that."

She stared at him in the shadows. "No," she said slowly. "You shouldn't have."

"I'll not forget myself again," he promised. "You needn't worry."

"I won't," she said, quietly.

They resumed their walk along the cliff's edge without saying anything. The cliff jutted in to be nearer the house and Anita noticed a wooden stairway with railings on either side of it leading from the edge down to the beach. It descended at intervals with platforms between each level; the final flight of wooden stairs ended on the narrow beach.

They halted by the steps and she said, "Is that the best way to the beach?"

"The only way," he told her. "There's a small wharf down below. But no one goes down there much except Pat. I haven't time for swimming when I take care of my shop."

"Yet you must get a great deal of satisfaction out of it," she said.

"It's my life!" he said with unexpected

passion. "I'd never let anything come be-tween the shop and me."

"I've always had an interest in antiques," she went on. "But I know so little about them I'll be ashamed to visit your place."

He laughed. "You needn't be. There are only certain basics for the beginner to learn." He paused. "Come to think. I happen to have a beginner's book in my car right now. I got it back from a cus-tomer today and I left it on the seat. If you'll wait here a minute I'll get it for you."

"Don't bother!" she protested.

"It's a pleasure," he said. "I'd like to see you with enough knowledge of what I'm doing to be able to move around the shop and discuss the pieces intelligently with me."

"I doubt if reading a book would take me that far."

"You'd be surprised," he maintained, "this one is excellent. There are loads of il-lustrations. When I take you back inside I'll give you some tips on it."

His enthusiasm was too great to be de-nied. She said, "All right. I'll be happy to borrow it. Only don't expect too much."

"I'll go across to my car," he said. "Be back in a minute." And he hurried away in the darkness leaving her standing not far from the steps to the steep embankment to the beach.

At first she felt all right. It was only as the seconds passed that she began to glance uneasily about in the darkness. She wished Gordon would soon return and wondered just how far away his car was. Involuntarily she gazed across the wide expanse of lawn to the darkened windows of Shorecliff. There were still no lights showing on the ground floor. Mary Vane must be murmuring her incantations and attempting to conjure up the apparition of Amanda.

A chill shot through her and it wasn't the cool of the night that caused it — but rather an overwhelming sense of impending danger. It was a feeling she had known before — one she associated with the black-shrouded figure and eerie pink face of the ghostly Amanda. The night was still but all at once there came a sudden sighing of wind. Panic welled up in her as she turned quickly and saw that she was no longer alone!

The phantom form of the long dead Amanda was approaching her, the porcelain face standing out weirdly in the darkness.

CHAPTER FIVE

Anita shrank back with a cry of fear. The apparition with the shining porcelain death mask was between her and the path. And as it advanced steadily she turned and fled toward the brink of the cliff. Looming as a means of escape were the rickety wooden stairs to the beach below.

Her footsteps thudded on the soft grass as she raced toward the stairs. A single glance backward served to let her know the phantom was still at her heels. She grasped the wooden railing and started down the steps. In the darkness she had no idea where the first landing might be. And then something tripped her. With a wild scream and outstretched hands she went toppling forward.

Falling through space, she had visions of crashing all the way to the rocky beach below. But her drop was short and she landed on what must have been the first of the several platforms. The impact of her body as she hit the rough wooden planking caused her to temporarily black out. She had no idea how long she lay there in a faint. When she came to her entire body was bruised and aching. For a moment she did not stir. Then she raised herself on her elbow with a tiny moan.

The wash of the waves on the beach below was her only reply. And then far off a gull sent a haunting cry into the night. She drew a deep breath that was partly a sob. Glancing up toward the stairs above, her terrified eyes searched for some sign of the ghost of Amanda which had brought her to this sad state. There was only the blackness and the stars far above.

Now she stirred some more and made an effort to stand. She was still afraid she might have broken some bones. But it seemed she had been luckier than she could have hoped. She had not so much as sprained an ankle. She stood very still for a long moment and then groped for the railing and slowly began to climb back toward the top. She'd only gone a few steps when she brushed against something. It was a chain of some sort that had been stretched across the stairs from railing to railing at a height of about six or seven inches. So that was what had tripped her!

She stepped over it and continued on up.

Then she heard Gordon's voice from above. "Anita! Where are you?" His shout was anxious.

Resting a moment she called back, "Down here!"

A few seconds later she heard him coming down the stairs to meet her. When they met, he asked, "What happened?"

She was trembling and almost ill. She leaned weakly against him. "After you left I saw her! Amanda!"

"What?"

"Yes," she insisted. "I was wondering what was keeping you and about to go back on my own."

"I couldn't find the book," Gordon said. "Then I decided someone must have taken it into the house. I went in and found it on the hall table."

"There was a weird rustle of wind. I turned and saw her face! The porcelain face! She was coming toward me!"

"Why didn't you shout for me?"

"She was between me and the house. All I could think of was getting away from her. I ran to the stairs and started down. Something tripped me and I fell to the first platform."

His arm tightened around her for support. His tone was grim. "You might have fallen further than that. It's a miracle you weren't killed!"

"I know," she said. "There's a chain stretched across the stairs."

"A chain?" his tone was incredulous.

"Something! I don't know!" She was too weary to think and her body ached from head to toe.

"Can you manage the rest of the way?" he asked. "I want to get you back to the house and let them get the doctor."

"I'll be all right," she protested although she felt far from it.

"After a fall like that you must have medical attention," he said. "No telling what harm may have been done."

He supported her and they quickly went up the last of the stairs. When they reached the top she stood for a moment knowing how weak and shaken she was. Her eyes wandered to the old mansion and she saw all the lights were on in the lower part of Shorecliff once more.

She said, "The seance must have ended."

"Apparently," Gordon said bitterly.

"I wonder if they contacted Amanda," she said. "I know she was here."

Before Gordon could answer, the tall

figure of her husband loomed out of the darkness and came striding toward them. Charles' handsome face looked sullen.

"What happened to you two?" he demanded.

Gordon spoke up, "Anita had a bad fall. It's lucky she isn't lying down at the bottom of the stairs dead."

"The stairs?" Charles stared at her. "What were you doing on the stairs?"

"It doesn't matter now," Gordon said. "Get her back to the house and call Dr. Wilson."

Charles needed no further urging but quickly swept her up in his arms. She recognized her husband's superior strength and size in comparison to the slim, small stature of Gordon. The unhappy Gordon had been able to offer her no more help than to allow her to lean on him for support.

As Charles marched across the lawn with her, he asked again, "Why were you on the stairs?"

Knowing it would sound ridiculous, she said, "Amanda's ghost chased me down there."

"What?"

"It's true," she said. "She came toward me from the shadows. Gordon had left me alone for a moment. She was all in black and I saw that awful artificial face. It seemed to glow!"

"You must have let your nerves get the better of you," her husband commented. "You should have stayed for the seance."

"Did you reach Amanda?"

"Mary Vane's guide spoke for her. Only for a moment. Amanda claims she is still earthbound, unable to leave Shorecliff."

Then Charles was carrying her inside and the others crowded around them, Aunt Clem making high-pitched excited comments, Mary Vane speaking in her odd hollow voice of the shadow over the house and its occupants, and Pat giving instructions in her clear, ringing tones to Mrs. Miller, telling her to summon Dr. Wilson at once.

Anita continued to protest she didn't need the doctor but no one paid the slightest attention to her. Charles deposited her on their bed and Pat and Mrs. Miller came up to help her change into her night things.

When she was safely in bed, Mrs. Miller left and Pat stood by waiting for the doctor to come. The brown-haired girl gave her a knowing look. "You'd have done better to remain in the house," she said.

Anita closed her eyes as she relaxed on her pillow. "I couldn't face it," she said. "There is something odd and sinister about that Mary Vane. The whole thing is so unhealthy."

"She did reach her guide and Amanda spoke to us through Elsie."

"So I heard," Anita said in a tired voice. She opened her eyes and stared up at Pat. "What did you make of it?"

"It was spooky and convincing. Amanda claims she's bound to this place. She hinted only vindication of the murder will free her. That it must be settled."

Anita smiled bitterly. "Sounds as if Mary Vane concocted a message to please my husband."

Pat raised an eyebrow. "You're saying she's a fake?"

"I'm saying her message suited the situation," Anita said. "I'll vouch that Amanda's ghost is here. I saw her."

"Oh?" Pat sounded doubtful.

Then Dr. Wilson arrived and ended their conversation. Pat left the room to the doctor, Charles and her. But Anita noticed the quick glance of understanding that passed between Pat and Charles before she closed the door behind her.

Dr. Wilson's thin face showed concern

113

as he went about making a routine examination to discover the extent of her injuries. He wound up with the conclusion that she had reached on her own. She was badly bruised but otherwise in good shape. He seemed more upset about what had preceded the accident than the accident itself.

"This ghost you saw," he said. "Your account makes it seem much like the phantom figure you claim attacked you the night of your convulsion."

"It was the same one. Amanda Shore's ghost."

The doctor looked embarrassed. "Yes. I'm familiar with the Amanda Shore legend."

Charles, who had remained silent now said, "I think she's overwrought and allowing the ghost story to upset her."

Dr. Wilson nodded thoughtfully. "It could well be."

Anita raised herself in the bed. "But I *did* see Amanda."

Dr. Wilson frowned. "You were just as sure of that before. I'm afraid you've had another of your seizures. It may be necessary for you to seek some psychiatric help."

"There's nothing wrong with my mind!" she protested angrily.

"You wouldn't be aware of it if there was," Dr. Wilson reminded her in an easy tone. "We'll give you a few days bed rest and see how you come around."

Charles nodded approval. "I agree she needs more rest," he said.

Anita saw that it would be useless to argue with either of them. They were both so smugly certain that she was hysterical. The doctor murmured something about having a prescription sent and left. Charles saw him out and then returned to sit on her bedside. She was startled at the worn look on his face; his eyes seemed strangely bright.

He stared at her. "I'm very worried about you, Anita," he said.

"You needn't be."

"This business of your having these spells can't be allowed to go on without further looking into," he said. "Dr. Wilson agrees with me on that."

She sighed. "Let us wait until tomorrow to discuss that."

"You always put me off," he protested.

"What about the seance? Was it a success?"

He looked guarded. "In a limited way."

"Under what conditions did Mary Vane conduct it?"

Charles seemed vaguely startled by her question. "The usual, I guess," he said. "The room was in pitch blackness. We all sat around the table. At first we joined hands. Then as the seance progressed we were on our own."

"What went on?"

"There were long periods of silence," he said, as if remembering for himself. "Then Mary Vane would moan and call out to Elsie. That's the little girl who is her guide."

"I know."

"Next she began to moan loudly and an entirely different voice came from her lips. A little girl's voice. She seemed to be mixed up for a time. Then she said she was standing by Amanda. And Amanda claimed she was bound to this house by the rumors she was a murderess. As Elsie's voice faded, Mary Vane began to moan again and later asked for the lights to be turned on. She was white and completely exhausted from the strain of it all."

Anita gave him a searching look. "Do you believe it was really Amanda who gave you that message?"

He hesitated in replying, then said, "Yes. I think so."

"If you're so ready to believe you heard

from Amanda why are you so skeptical about my seeing her?"

Charles looked startled. "That's different!" he protested.

"I can't see how."

"One is hysteria and the other is serious spiritualistic experiment."

"I see," she sighed resignedly. She reached out and touched her hand to his. "Charles, I love you. But if we remain here and things like this go on I don't know what's going to happen to our love."

His eyes showed torment. "You know I'm worried about you."

"But you won't give up the idea of the book. You won't abandon Amanda?"

"You put that in such an odd way," he protested. "I can only assume Dr. Wilson is right. You are suffering from some form of hysteria."

"All right, Charles," she said quietly. "Let's stop discussing it for now. I'm very tired."

He leaned over and kissed her. Then he held her hand in his for a long moment with his eyes fixed gravely on her. "I'm as much puzzled about all this confusion between us as you are," he confessed. "But it has to be all right. I'm going downstairs to say goodnight to the others and tell them you're better."

When she was alone in the shadowed old bedroom her eyes brimmed with tears. For just a moment she had sensed the old Charles breaking through the shell of the obsessed man her husband had become. Their love had almost broken the spell Amanda had cast over him — but not quite. So it would continue, this unequal battle between herself and the century-dead-murderess for the possession of Charles.

Or was she battling with someone among the living? Once again she felt the circumstances were suspicious. According to Charles' account the living room had been in darkness most of the time of the seance. And those seated at the table had not been in contact with one another after the opening minutes of the weird ritual. How easy it would have been for Pat or even Aunt Clem to slip away from the table to don a disguise and appear on the lawn as Amanda's ghost. Even Mary Vane might have managed to absent herself for a brief period without the others being aware. There had been moments of silence, periods extending for quite a time according to the account Charles had given her.

In a way she would have been comforted to know that her adversary was mortal flesh. That she might have only a human to stand up against in this struggle. Pat was the most likely suspect — Pat who openly admired Charles and encouraged him against her whenever she could. But Anita was by no means sure.

Each time she'd been confronted by the apparition there had been an evil something about the figure that had forced all thought from her mind that it might be one of the others pretending. The atmosphere of horror in which the phantom with the porcelain face was wrapped left little question that she'd seen the real thing! So Amanda was bound to the house by the rumors concerning the murder! And it was likely she would continue to do so now that her evil domination had made Charles her slave.

Anita closed her eyes. Things were closing in too tightly to try and seek out a solution in her exhausted state. She would wait until the morning.

But when the morning came, bringing with it fog and rain, she found herself in no better mood.

Mrs. Miller brought up her meals on a tray since the doctor's orders about remaining in bed had been strict. She received little comfort from the dour housekeeper who seemed to regard the extra task of bringing up the trays as an affront to her.

Anita was curious about the woman's attitude toward the house in which she worked and the family she served. She asked, "Do you agree with the others that Shorecliff is haunted?"

Mrs. Miller sniffed. "I've seen no ghosts to scare me here. Though I can't say the same about some of the living."

She glanced up from her tray with a wan smile. "You don't sound too fond of the Shores."

Mrs. Miller's leathery face showed scorn as she stood by the bed. "Clare was uppity and Clem is the most selfish of them all. She's ruined her son's life and is not above worse. Shorecliff has always been a wicked place. Not much wonder the evil spirits hover here."

"Yet you've lived and worked here for years," Anita said. "Why, if you dislike the family and the house so much?"

"Some folk have small choice," the old woman said bitterly.

Anita considered this, taking in her own case. "I wonder," she said in a quiet tone. "Or do we make prisoners of ourselves?"

"We are what we are," Mrs. Miller commented, "and nothing can change that!" And she stalked out.

Anita stared after her with puzzled eyes. Once again she was filled with a conviction that there was something behind Mrs. Miller's bitterness, some unrevealed secret. The housekeeper's attitude toward them was not what it should be. She made no pretense about her feelings and yet she was tolerated by Pat and the others.

Pat usually called by the room several times during the day and evening. When she came that night Anita determined to try and get some information from her. This was never easy.

Pat entered the bedroom casually and informed her, "Charles has found some letters in a box that date back almost to Amanda's time. He's going over them in the library now."

"I thought something must be keeping him down there."

"You're looking much better," Pat observed. She was wearing a bright red mini-dress. She stood there with the poise of one who knew she was capable of drawing admiring male glances.

Anita sat up in bed. "I plan to get up tomorrow."

"Did the doctor give you permission?"

"It's only a day earlier than he suggested."

Pat warned her. "I doubt if Charles will approve."

Anita looked at her grimly. She was sure Pat would prefer having her confined to her bed. It gave her more scope to exert her own charms on Charles. She said, "I'll take that chance."

"He's very worried about you," Pat said. "And I don't think he's too well himself. He's so nervous all the time."

Anita looked at the other girl. "You know about his accident. He was still taking treatments for the head injuries he received until just a few weeks before we left Boston."

"Perhaps he should talk to a doctor about himself."

Anita smiled bitterly. "You might be able to convince him of that. All he can talk about to me is my hysteria."

"It is too bad," Pat commented noncommittally.

Anita then brought up the subject that had been on her mind. "I've seen a lot of Mrs. Miller since my illness. I find her a strange person."

Pat nodded. "She is odd."

"And beyond her peculiar manner I notice that she is curt and overbearing. Not only toward me but with you and everyone else."

"I guess it is pretty obvious," Pat admitted with a smile.

"She's bitter about the family and calls this a wicked house."

"That sounds like her."

Anita stared at her. "You seem to think nothing of this?"

"I do. But perhaps I understand."

"You're one of the family. Even though you were adopted. You must have some notion of why she feels free to act this way."

"I have."

"Then there is a reason?"

"Yes," Pat said. "I suppose you have a right to know, since you and Charles are now the owners here."

"It wasn't my intention to pry," Anita told her. "But I am puzzled."

The other girl gave her a wise look. "She feels she has a right to be here."

"She has been employed in the house a long while," Anita agreed.

"There's more to it than that," Pat said meaningfully. "She would have the same rights to this property as Clare and Clem if she were legitimate."

It came as a shock. Anita stared at the brown-haired girl. "You mean she has Shore blood?"

"Take another good look at her next time she comes up," Pat said in a jeering tone. "She looks almost enough like Aunt Clem to be a sister. Except her skin has been weathered by outdoor life and rough work while Aunt Clem's is white."

Anita at once pictured the two old women and realized there was a likeness. "But if this is generally known isn't it embarrassing to have her around here?"

"In the beginning Aunt Clem's father saw that Mrs. Miller and her husband had one of the farms owned by the estate. Then when Miller died and the property was sold he insisted she be brought here as housekeeper. No one was able to stand up to the old man from what I've heard. So she was installed as housekeeper and remained on after his death."

"Does she have any children?" she asked.

Pat nodded. "A son and daughter and a few grandchildren. They all live and work in Pennbridge."

"And she was left nothing by the Shores?"

Pat smiled bitterly. "She isn't officially recognized by them. Beyond what amounts to a lifetime job she has been given nothing. So she does feel resentment. Perhaps I annoy her more than anyone else, since I was adopted."

"No wonder she claims it's an unhappy house," Anita reflected.

"If I were in her place I'd never have stayed here," the other girl said. "But she prefers to remain and flaunt her claim to equality with the rest of us."

Anita thought about this long after Pat had gone back downstairs. Now she clearly understood why Mrs. Miller behaved the way she did. The strange, dour manner was her way of letting the family know she considered herself as good as any of them although she had only the official status of an employee.

It also started another trend of thought in Anita's mind. Wouldn't Mrs. Miller be a prime suspect for the role of her attacker? Mrs. Miller who sought vengeance on the Shore family and who would be certain to resent Charles for inheriting half of Shore-cliff. Could she have succumbed to a kind of madness and be playing the role of Amanda's ghost to frighten them off? It was a possibility although not too likely a one.

That night Charles came up to bed close to midnight. He looked so worn she was more fearful of his mental state than ever. He appeared especially aloof and lost in his thoughts.

She asked him, "Make any worthwhile discoveries in those letters?"

He paused in removing his shirt to frown at her. "Who told you about them?"

"Pat."

"Oh!" This seemed to make a difference. He went on into the bathroom to wash and put on his pajamas.

When he returned, she said, "You didn't tell me about the letters."

He shrugged. "Nothing much to tell. Those people were pretty biased in their views. Nearly everyone of them spoke of Amanda as being the one who killed that captain."

"Isn't that the view that has come down through the years?"

His burning eyes fixed on her angrily. "I don't think it is fair to Amanda. I still hope I'll be able to prove her innocent."

"I hope you're able to," she said quietly. "But I don't think you should upset yourself so much about it."

"What difference does it make to you?" he asked sharply.

She gazed at the angry, handsome man standing by the bed in his pajamas and wondered if the wide gulf that had come between them could ever be spanned. Charles was a different person from the affable young man who had driven down from Boston. Was it purely the evil spell of Amanda or was his mental health slowly breaking down? And his obsession with the dead woman merely a coincidence? She wished she knew.

The next day was warm and pleasant again. Anita dressed and went down for breakfast. Her appearance was greeted with raised eyebrows and a frown of rebuke from Charles. But she placated him so well she even gained permission from him to use their car and go into the village.

She left soon after breakfast, fearful that Charles might think it over and change his mind. She was not only desperately anxious to get away from the gloom of Shorecliff but she wanted to have a private talk with Gordon. He was the only one she had to turn to now and she was coming to value his friendship more each day.

Carefully following the road they had first taken when they came to Pennbridge she drove back to the antique shop. She parked the sports car in the yardway and went inside.

She was greeted by a tall, pimply youth with a mop of golden hair that flowed over his ears and collar. She asked the gawky teen-ager where Gordon was. "You can tell him it's Mrs. Charles Shore."

The youth looked at her with skepticism on his sharp young face. "Can't say he'll come down," he said. "He's working on a rush upholstery order in the attic."

She smiled. "Give him my message anyway."

The boy went reluctantly and Anita was left alone in the musty quiet of the cluttered area, surrounded by shelves and stacks of antiques. Just ahead of her were a couple of Governor Winthrop desks in seemingly good condition. She'd been studying Gordon's book and was beginning to be able to identify certain pieces. Wedgwood of the rare old blue pattern, plaster figures of another era, picture frames and painted china door knobs were on display. There were a number of pieces of Victorian furniture and some that she suspected were a good deal older. A sleepy air of other days hovered about the shadowed display area.

There were the sound of footsteps on the

rear stairs and Gordon appeared in shirt-sleeves and a leather work apron. The gawky boy was behind him.

Gordon came straight over to her. "I'm surprised to see you around so soon," he said.

"I felt well enough so I got up."

"Good for you," he said. "Come into my office."

She hesitated. "I know you're busy. I don't want to hold you back."

"Don't worry about that. I'm my own boss and I have plenty of time." He led her through cluttered aisles to a door that opened into a small but neat office.

"My inner sanctum," he said, a smile on his thin face. "Sit down."

She sat in a plain chair which was of an early period and delightfully comfortable. She looked around the tiny office with its desk, phone and filing cabinet. "This is nice," she said.

"I like it," he agreed, sitting back in the chair behind the desk. "Mind if I have some orange juice? Would you care to join me?"

"No thank you," she said. "But you go right ahead."

He rummaged in a lower drawer of the desk and produced a can of orange juice and a tall glass. As he punched holes in the top of the can with an opener, he said, casually, "Perhaps I didn't mention it. But I happen to be a diabetic. This orange juice fits in with my insulin routine."

"I didn't know," she said, as he poured himself out a full glass.

"One of the minor annoyances of my life," he said. "I've learned to live with it." He took a mouthful of the drink and then asked, "How are you managing?"

"Not too well," she said. "I'm worried about Charles. He's very tense and not at all like his old self."

Gordon nodded. "I don't think he seems well either."

"Of course he puts everything down to my hysteria," she said, with a deep sigh. "Especially after my fall the other night."

"I know," Gordon agreed quietly. "By the way, you were right."

"Right about what?"

"There being a chain across those stairs. I went out the next morning and found it."

She frowned. "What was it doing there?"

"Now that's a mystery," he said. "It seemed like a deliberate trap laid for you or someone who was expected to rush down those steps. But who would have known that you were going to be frightened there by a ghost?"

She let her eyes meet his. "The ghost?"

The eyes behind his thick glasses showed a strange light. "It's odd you should say that," he said. "Because this was no ordinary chain. It came from a stone gate in the yard. It's always been there as far back as anyone at Shorecliff can remember. Used for keeping the horses from running off." He paused. "Well, someone or something used superhuman strength to pry that century-old chain from the gate just to drape it on those stairs as a trap."

Anita caught her breath. "It would date back to Amanda's time, then?"

He looked grave. "I suppose it would."

CHAPTER SIX

Anita stared at him across the desk. "How can she seem so real?" she asked desperately. "Have so much power after being dead a century?"

"I'm beginning to ask that question myself," he said.

"Who else but Amanda would pick that particular chain to use against me?"

Gordon's face was solemn. "I couldn't help thinking that same thing," he said. As he put aside the empty glass and told her, "It's that medium, Mary Vane. She's got us all believing in this nonsense."

"I'm not so sure it's nonsense," she said, deadly serious.

Gordon seemed startled. "You mustn't allow yourself to become frightened," he warned her.

"If it wasn't a ghost the other night it had to be someone from the house."

He furrowed his brow. "You're sure you didn't hear an unexpected sound and imagine you saw someone?"

"I'm positive."

Gordon shrugged. "In that case you have to suspect somebody at Shorecliff or settle for a ghost. I'd say it would be more normal to suspect someone."

"But perhaps not as close to the truth."

"Who would you suspect?"

"Anyone who was at that seance," she said. "Most likely Pat, but it could have been your mother or Mary Vane."

"I don't see Mother as all that agile," he said with a grim smile.

"Or it might have been someone else whom I hadn't thought of until lately. Someone who wasn't at the seance. Mrs. Miller."

"Mrs. Miller?"

"Yes, I know her history now. And it seems to me she might decide to take out some of her hatred against the Shores by tormenting me."

He smiled thinly. "An ingenious thought. But I doubt if it has any importance to a solution of your problem."

Anita persisted, "But it could have been her."

"I suppose so."

She gave him a significant look. "That still leaves Pat the most likely suspect. Especially since she's clearly infatuated with my husband."

"Do you think Charles has paid any attention to her?"

"I can't be sure," she admitted. "I know he enjoys having her admiration. She isn't exactly homely."

"Not exactly," Gordon agreed with a rueful smile.

"So I guess we'll have to leave it there for the moment."

"Maybe," he said reluctantly. "I do believe you should be extremely careful. Since these attempts have been made against you it's pretty certain you're a target for someone. And it's only a matter of time until they'll try to get at you again."

"Not a very pleasant outlook."

"But we have to be realistic," Gordon warned her.

"What can I do?"

He gave her a wary glance. "I think you should protect yourself. I'm only sorry there isn't some direct means of passage from Mother's side of the house to yours. But since there isn't keep my phone number near you."

"I will," she promised.

"I'll come any time you call me," he went on earnestly. "Even phone me here if you need me."

She smiled her gratitude. "Thank you, Gordon."

He brushed her thanks aside with one of his thin artistic hands and rose from behind the desk to pace uneasily. "I don't think I'm being any particular help at a time when you most need assistance."

"You're my one friend at Shorecliff," she said.

He paused in his pacing and gazed at her sadly. "If only I'd met you before Charles."

She gave a forlorn laugh. "It's too late to worry about that."

"That's the way it has always been with me. The things I could really care about always come to me when it's too late."

"You have your work," she reminded him. "And your home."

"You know what I put up with at home," he said. "My mother makes me continually miserable."

"I'm sorry," she said.

He slicked back a loose lock of dark hair and changed his manner. "But we're not concerned about me. You're the one in danger." He paused. "I hate to say this. But I think Charles is playing a major role in whatever is wrong."

She frowned in astonishment. "You

think Charles would plot to harm me?"

"Not the Charles you married. But the Charles who is at Shorecliff at this moment," he said, standing directly before her in the tiny office.

"I know he's upset and tense," she agreed. "But I don't believe he'd hurt me."

"Many a murdered wife has said those very words."

"Murdered!" she echoed.

He nodded. "I think Charles is in a state of mental unbalance. It may be the result of his accident, or to be utterly fantastic he could be under the influence of the evil Amanda, or being somewhat more practical it's possible he's become infatuated with Pat and together they're planning to eliminate you."

It was so close to what she'd been thinking herself she found the frank declaration terrifying. Swallowing hard, she said, "No matter what you think, I'm not in danger from my husband."

"I've known cousin Charles a great deal longer than you," Gordon said. "And taking everything into consideration I say yes. And I say it emphatically."

"What can I do?"

"You could leave him and Shorecliff."

"No."

"Or try to stand by and see what is behind all this."

"That is what I must do," she said.

"In that case you'll have to protect yourself."

"How?"

Gordon looked at her solemnly. "Do you have a gun of any kind? Does Charles have one?"

"I don't think so. Not that I know of." They were moving into an area which had no reality for her. Until now she'd never been faced with a situation where a weapon might be considered useful. She'd never expected to be discussing such a thing.

The young antique dealer's eyes were grave. "You should arm yourself."

"Oh, no!" she protested.

"Why not? These attacks against you could have cost you your life."

"I just can't face the idea."

"You'd better think about it," he said. "I have. And all you have to do is say the word and I'll get you a gun of some kind. It's perfectly all right for you to have something to protect yourself."

"Give me time to think about it," she said unhappily.

He spread his hands in a gesture of resignation. "I can't force a gun on you. I can only tell you I think you should have one."

"What good is a gun against a phantom like Amanda?"

"The answer might be surprising," he said grimly. "You've admitted you're not certain if you're dealing with a ghost or someone pretending to be one."

"I know," she faltered.

"If I were going to give you honest advice I should tell you to go to the police. They should be notified about these happenings at Shorecliff. I discussed that with Mother this morning and naturally she was horrified at the idea. She accused me of wanting to scandalize the family name."

"It is a weird story," she said.

"But you have been attacked," Gordon pointed out.

"I know. But the police aren't liable to be too receptive to my stories about a phantom with a porcelain face," she said.

Gordon shrugged. "You can only tell them what you believe. If that's what you believe you shouldn't be ashamed to discuss it with the proper authorities. But if you do, don't let on to Mother that I advised it."

Anita got up with a rueful smile on her pretty face. "I'll be careful about that. At the moment I can't picture myself going to the police."

"In case you do," Gordon said, "I'd advise the State Police at Portsmouth. There's an Inspector Harry Decker there who is a level-headed young man."

"I'll remember," she promised. "And thanks again."

He took her by the arm and walked to the door with her. "I don't know what Mary Vane is up to," he said. "But yesterday she and Mother drove into Pennbridge to the library. According to Mother she loaded up on books about local history."

They were out in the main shop again with its odors of ancient furniture, polish stain and just plain dust. She gave Gordon a worried glance. "She must be getting ready to hold more seances. Probably to impress Charles with her knowledge of local history."

He nodded grimly. "Don't be surprised if her guide, little Elsie, should come up with some interesting historical accounts of the area."

The gawky youth stared at her openly as Gordon led her to the door. She had an idea few young women visited the antique dealer and his assistant was consequently impressed.

She paused at the door to say, "We talked about so many other things you didn't get around to showing me any Duncan Phyfe or Regency pieces."

"I'm afraid we haven't much here right now aside from Early Colonial New England items. You can come back later to see them. That will give you a good reason," he suggested with a smile.

"I'll do that," she promised.

"I hope what I've said hasn't alarmed you too much," Gordon said with great sincerity.

"Of course not. I know you meant it for the best."

"Believe that. I had to speak frankly. There are not too many chances at the house."

She said goodbye and as she drove away, he was still standing in the doorway of the antique shop. His slender figure in the leather apron had a strangely appealing effect on her. He looked like a lonely, unhappy boy and he really wasn't much more than that. Travelling back along the narrow road leading to Shorecliff she reviewed all he'd said.

His admission of love for her had been touching. She liked him a great deal and if there hadn't been Charles to consider she could easily imagine herself falling in love with him. But there was Charles! At least for the moment.

After what Gordon had said to her just now she began to wonder just how long her marriage might last — and how the end would come. There was no question that Gordon was seriously worried about her safety or he wouldn't have offered to supply her with a gun.

A gun to protect her against Charles!

The idea seemed grotesquely fantastic at first thought. But then she had to see things as they were, not as she liked to fondly remember them. Charles was no longer the ideal husband. He was confused or worse. And he had managed to suggest she was the one with a hysterical nature. There was no question that Dr. Wilson had believed it from the night of her convulsion attack.

And that attack brought up another delicate point. She could still recall the stinging pain of the weapon the phantom had plunged in her arm. And she felt sure it had caused the convulsive symptoms. But no one would listen to her. Not Charles! Not the doctor! No one!

She had no friend to stand by her except Gordon. She must depend on him more and more. At the same time she wanted to hide their growing friendship from the others — especially his mother and Pat who would be bound to work against them if they found out.

As she headed the car through the stone gates of the estate she saw the twin houses of Shorecliff standing in lonely dignity. How much had taken place there! The mere account of the generations of Shores who had lived and died in the mansions would make a fascinating story. In a way she could understand why Charles was attracted to putting down Amanda's colorful life.

What alarmed her was his obsession with the dead woman and the change that had come over him. These thoughts ran through her mind as she parked the car in the rear of the house and walked around to the front door.

Charles and Mary Vane were standing under the white portico, deep in conversation. As she mounted the several steps the medium turned and gave her a rather unpleasant stare.

"I see you are able to drive again," she said in her odd hollow voice.

"Yes," Anita said with quiet curtness.

"Then you should feel well enough to

join us in our seance tonight," Mary Vane said with a cold smile on her gaunt, lovely face. "The conditions are favorable and I believe this is our great opportunity."

"Anita is not interested in our explorations of the spirit world," Charles said, a touch of annoyance in his voice.

She decided to surprise him. With an air of amazement, she said, "Why do you say that, Charles? I've always taken an interest in whatever you might be doing." And turning to the medium, she added, "Of course I'll take part in the seance this evening. What time do you plan to have it and where?"

"We felt it should be at Mrs. Morehouse's tonight," the medium said. "And it is best to wait for complete darkness. The spirits respond more readily. So we'll not begin until nine-thirty."

"I'll come with Charles," Anita promised, having the feeling that her quick acceptance had not pleased Mary Vane very much.

The dark woman inclined her head slightly. "I trust you will find it rewarding," she said. And then with a special smile for Charles, added, "Until nine-thirty then." And she walked down the steps to cross to the entrance of the adjoining house.

The sun was just reaching the front lawn area. Anita leaned against one of the big white columns of the verandah and smiled at her husband. "Judging by your reactions I don't believe I'm particularly wanted at that seance."

Charles, looking as haggard as ever, scowled at her. "I'd like you to go in a serious frame of mind."

"But I am serious!" she protested.

He shook his head. "I know how you feel about this Amanda business. And I know when you're deliberately trying to taunt me."

"You're so wrong," she said.

His burning eyes fixed on her. "I ask you one thing."

"What?"

"Don't come tonight unless you are in a mood to believe."

"All right," she said. "I'll come with an open mind. Does that satisfy you?"

"I'll let you know later," he said. "After the seance." And he turned and went inside without waiting for her or saying anything else.

She felt hurt. Even when she went out of her way to go along with his madness he didn't seem especially pleased. His sullen resentment of her and everything she did

144

was becoming terrifying. With a sigh she followed him inside.

Dinner was a dull, difficult interlude and she found filling in the time afterward even harder. She was too nervous to read yet there was little else to do. Pat had vanished somewhere and Charles had retired to the library, no doubt to prepare himself for the seance. She strolled in the garden until dusk began to fall. With the approach of darkness she became nervous out there alone and returned to the house.

A cloak of silence had fallen over the old house, almost as if in anticipation of the weird ritual soon to be performed — as if the ancient mansion was anticipating the return of Amanda Shore. She slowly made her way into the living room and over to the portrait of the supposed murderess. Once again she was struck by the arrogant beauty of the lovely girl of long ago.

The complacency of Amanda's expression was in strict contrast to the chill rage in her eyes. Those eyes gleamed with an unconcealed hatred and contempt. She felt that cold clamminess surge about her once more and she hastily turned away from the troublesome painting and rushed out of the room.

She found herself on the stairs, but she

didn't want to go to her bedroom. And she realized she had not yet been taken on a tour of the house by Pat or Mrs. Miller. Though she was supposedly mistress of Shorecliff she knew very little about it.

Why wouldn't this be a suitable moment to visit the third and fourth levels? It seemed an ideal way to fill in the time despite growing shadows that were settling down on stairs and corridors. She moved swiftly along the hallways of the third floor and saw from occasional open doorways that the size and decor of the bedrooms up there were similar to those on her own level.

Then she climbed up the steeper stairway to the fourth floor. It occupied less area because of the mansard roof, and the hallways were narrower. Most of the doors to the various rooms were open; only one or two had any furniture in them. At the very end of one of the corridors she came to a room with nothing but a huge mirror, mounted in a wooden frame and almost a foot taller than she was. It had a slightly smoky look that suggested it might need renewing but there could be no doubt that it was a magnificent example of an old-fashioned mirror. No doubt many beauties of another age had surveyed themselves in its surface, she thought, as she studied her own reflection.

The room was already misted with the approaching darkness. She knew it was time to go back downstairs, but the mirror held her fascinated. And then, almost without her realizing it, the air about her began to be suffused with the rich perfume of Attar of Roses.

And joining her in the mirror was the same terrifying figure of Amanda that had stalked her so many times before!

Anita was frozen motionless with horror. As though hypnotized, she continued to stare into the dim reflection of herself and the phantom in the mirror — and saw the hand of the porcelain-faced Amanda raised in that poised gesture, as if to strike her.

Remembering the stabbing pain of the other night broke her spell. She cried out fearfully, dodged and wheeled around. As she did the phantom vanished in the corridor and she was left alone and whimpering in the nearly dark room.

It was a full moment before she dared venture out into the corridor. She could see no sign of the weird figure. Her heart pounded as she raced for the stairs. She had almost reached the bottom when an austere female form emerged from the shadows to face her.

It was the grim Mrs. Miller.

"Oh, it was you up there," the house-keeper said sourly. "I heard footsteps and couldn't imagine who it might be."

Still grasping the bannister Anita came down the remaining steps. "I was looking around."

"No one ever goes up there," the dour housekeeper said in her overbearing fashion.

"So I gather," Anita said, recovering herself a little. "Most of the rooms are empty."

"Yes. Except those used for storage."

Anita stared at the unfriendly Mrs. Miller and wondered if she could have been playing the role of the ghost. It might have been her. She said, by way of testing her reaction, "One of the rooms has a magnificent mirror in it."

The housekeeper's face was devoid of any betraying expression. "Yes," she said dryly. "There are some say it once belonged to that Amanda. She was supposed to be a vain beauty."

"So I've heard," Anita said in a small voice.

"Her vanity is in the dust now," the old woman said with obvious satisfaction. "Along with the rest of her! The murdering hussy!" And with that she left Anita and vanished along a corridor that went to the rear of the old building.

Anita stood there a moment, shaken and astonished. It was impossible to make up her mind whether Mrs. Miller was the ghost who'd threatened her. Her remark that the mirror had once belonged to Amanda added to the chill remembrance of the scary moment. She quickly made her way downstairs as it was time to attend the seance.

Charles was impatiently waiting for her. He glanced at his wrist watch. "You're late as usual," he said. "Pat has gone on ahead."

She found her voice again as she joined him. "I was exploring upstairs," she said.

He frowned. "What's up there?"

"A good many things. A huge mirror Mrs. Miller claims once belonged to Amanda, to name one."

Charles looked startled. "Did you see it?"

"Of course," she said.

He stood there hesitantly. "I'd go up and take a look now but I don't want to keep the others waiting."

She smiled. "The mirror has been up there a hundred years. It should keep until the seance is over."

He glanced longingly towards the stairs and then at her. "I suppose you're right," he said reluctantly. "But I must go up there later."

They crossed the lawn to the house next door. The others were already grouped around a table in the living room. Anita was cheered to see that Gordon was there.

When they were seated, Mary Vane, more imposing than ever in a black velvet gown with a low neckline and drooping silver earrings, addressed them in her weird, echo of voice, "Tonight we shall attempt to contact the late Amanda Shore," she said. "If there are any of you not in the proper vibration I would urge you to leave before we begin."

Anita was still numb and weak from the experience she'd had in the other part of the house. She glanced at Charles, seated next to her. His handsome face showed tension and weariness and he stared straight ahead. On her right was Aunt Clem, an eager, anticipatory smile animating her pale face. Beyond that sat Gordon; he gave Anita an assuring smile that made her feel better at once. Avoiding the medium, she let her eyes wander to Pat who sat next to Charles and looked pleasantly confident.

The medium said, "Then we shall begin. Will you turn out the lights please?"

"Gordon!" Aunt Clem said in her irritable fashion. And her son rose obediently, if wearily, to do her bidding.

As soon as the lights were switched off the medium said, "Now will you all please clasp hands so the circle is completed!"

Anita reached out in the darkness and took Aunt Clem's cold, damp hand in hers and groped with the other until she found Charles' hand. The touch of his skin was so hot she worried that he might be suffering from some fever. Now the medium began to moan.

The moaning and gasping went on for some time. Anita found it nerve-wracking. Suddenly there was silence; there was not a word from Mary Vane. Anita heard someone moving their feet uneasily. Then Charles let go of her hand and so did Aunt Clem, leaving her feeling isolated and alone in the inky darkness.

All at once Mary Vane began to groan again and sob. Her fists hammered on the table as if she were in great agony. Anita was startled by the performance and decided that the medium was putting on a very convincing show.

Or was she actually making contact with the dead?

There was another moment of complete silence and then the voice of a child issued from the shadows, "I am Elsie," the child said. "And I have found Amanda."

A chill ran down Anita's spine. This was a voice she had never heard before. And it was a child's voice speaking in the fresh manner of a youngster. It was hard not to be impressed.

Charles spoke out in a tense voice. "Where is Amanda?"

"Here at Shorecliff," Elsie said brightly. "She is holding my hand. We are in the room with you all."

Charles spoke again. "Will Amanda tell us if she is happy?"

There was a silence. Then the childish voice said, "She is not happy."

"Why?" Charles asked.

"Because she is earthbound."

"Why is she earthbound?" Charles put the question quickly.

Elsie answered at once, "It is the murder."

"Will she tell us about it?" Charles asked.

There was a silence again. Then a low moan. After which Elsie spoke, "Amanda says she loved the young man very much."

"And what happened?" Charles asked in that same strained fashion.

"He was untrue to her," the spirit-child said.

"Did this make her angry?" Charles asked.

"She was very angry," the child said.

"Did she murder the young man?"

There was no reply. Not a murmur or a sound in the darkness.

Charles repeated the question nervously, "Did she murder the young man?"

There was another weird silence. Anita's heart pounded madly. She was caught up in the strange drama.

Charles again put the question, "Did Amanda murder the young man?"

And then out of the blackness came another voice, richly female and mature, "Do you know what love is, Charles Shore?"

After a shocked moment of silence Charles answered, "I believe so."

"So you do," the utterly feminine voice mocked him from the grave. "Or you would not have sought me out?"

"You haven't answered my question, Amanda. It is Amanda, isn't it?" Charles questioned, a tremor of excitement in his tone.

"I am Amanda." The voice was mocking.

"I want to help you," Charles pleaded.

"To release you. I will write your story and put all the rumors and lies to rest."

A ripple of weird laughter pierced the shadows. "Yes. You know love, Charles Shore. You are the only one fit to bear a proud name."

"Then tell me the truth," Charles begged.

"The truth?" Amanda mocked him.

"Let me defend you whatever you may have done," Charles said.

"Whatever I may have done?" the question was put in a softer tone.

"Yes."

"You are the one!" Amanda declared more strongly again. "I have waited long for you to come to Shorecliff."

"You need have no fear," Charles said.

"I do not fear you nor any man," Amanda said scornfully. "But I do seek rest. So you shall know the truth!"

"Were you a murderess?"

"Yes! Yes!" Amanda shrieked out.

It was Charles who moaned now. "You did kill him?"

"He shamed me before my friends and family. Before all the town. I plunged a knife into his back. He slumped to the carpet. I bent down quickly with my scarf to staunch the blood."

"And then?" Charles asked.

"I dragged him down to the wine cellar. After all the others had gone to bed. There was an old abandoned well down there. I dropped the body into it and put the wooden flooring back in place."

"But no one discovered the body," Charles said.

This time the weird laughter was low. "I persuaded my father the floor should be bricked over. All the wine cellar floor. And he had it done at once. I think he guessed."

"Is the body still there?"

"He was handsome and he was strong," Amanda wailed. "And you will find his bones. Nothing but his dried and yellow bones!"

There was silence as the eerie voice became hushed. Charles asked no more questions. Then there was a low moan from the spot where Mary Vane was conducting the seance.

And Pat screamed, "Turn on the lights! Please turn on the lights!"

CHAPTER SEVEN

Pat's cry for the lights broke the strange spell. Now there was a babble of voices as the others joined in. The lights came on and Anita noticed Gordon Morehouse had looked after them again. Mary Vane had slumped forward on the round table with her head resting on her arm. Her face was a ghastly white and her eyes were still closed.

Pat was on her feet and over by the medium. She touched a hand to the woman's motionless shoulder and then glanced nervously at them. "Do you think she's all right?"

Charles nodded. "She should come out of it in a moment." And he went across to stand by the other side of the medium.

Aunt Clem gave Anita a shocked look. "What a dreadful business! I shall never allow a seance in this house again."

Gordon laughed harshly. "Why not, Mother? Can't you bear to hear the truth occasionally?"

Aunt Clem's pinched white face showed disgust. "What kind of truth was that? The wanderings of a mad woman would be closer to it. Mary Vane must be insane to let such words come from her lips!"

"But those were spirit voices speaking," Anita reminded her.

Aunt Clem looked grim. "Anything that Mary Vane says I hold her responsible for! I don't care what voice the remarks may be couched in. I'll not have her inferring a Shore was a murderess."

"Mary Vane is your guest," Gordon reminded her.

"She won't be for long after this disgraceful business tonight," his mother emphatically replied.

Anita returned her attention to the medium again and saw that under the combined attentions of Pat and Charles she was beginning to show signs of reviving. Now she slowly raised her head and stared around the room with blank eyes.

"Did I reach her?" she asked in her own weirdly hollow voice, pitched low at this moment. "Did I get through to Amanda Shore?"

"Yes," Charles said, his face showing the strain of the seance.

The medium's dark-ringed eyes looked

at him. "Was Elsie able to give you her answers?"

Charles sighed. "Elsie dropped out of it early in the seance. I managed to directly question Amanda."

Mary Vane showed consternation. "Amanda broke through to you herself!"

"Yes."

The medium was putting on a good show, as good as the seance itself, if this was all pretense, Anita thought. The dark woman hesitated for a moment and gazed dully at them all.

Then she turned her attention to Charles again and questioned him, "Did you find out the truth?"

"I don't know," he said in a grave voice.

"Did she mention the murder?"

"Yes," he said. "She admitted to killing the young man."

Aunt Clem stepped forward, an angry look on her thin, pinched face. "We don't want any of that repeated," she shrieked. "It's all a lot of nonsense and mustn't be spread around."

Charles looked at her with weary eyes. "How can you conceal the truth?"

"But it's not the truth!" Aunt Clem exclaimed. "Just the ramblings of that woman!"

Mary Vane's eyes opened wide. And with a look of perplexity she turned to Charles again. "What did this Amanda say?"

"She claims the body is hidden in an old well in the cellar. And that the wooden floor was covered with bricks at her request. If she told the truth the body is still down there."

"A wicked lie!" Aunt Clem protested. "The body can't be down there! And I'll refuse to allow the wine cellar to be searched."

Gordon Morehouse laughed. "You've forgotten something, Mother. Amanda lived in the other house. And you have no say there!"

The old woman glared at her son and stood motionless for a moment, her thin hands clasped, her fingers working nervously. She gave Charles a pleading glance. "You won't play fast and loose with the family name, Charles," she begged. "You'll not go any further with this. We don't want the police involved."

"If we should discover the skeleton and be forced to advise the police I doubt that it would necessarily mean any publicity," Charles said.

"But of course it would!" Aunt Clem snapped. "Those reporters find out everything the police know."

Charles shrugged. "Then we'll have to take our chances. I intend to search the wine cellar."

Aunt Clem gasped and turned to Anita. "Can't you persuade him to be sensible about this?"

"I hardly think any body will be found," was all she could say.

Gordon spoke up quickly. "I agree. I think we're making a lot of fuss over nothing."

Mary Vane remained seated in her chair. She glared at the young man. "If Amanda spoke from the dead you should be willing to believe her. Any message she may have given is not to be taken lightly."

Charles addressed himself to the medium. "Don't worry! I'm following this up." And he glanced at Anita. "We'll be going back to the house now."

She was not surprised that he'd decided to leave so suddenly. She was sure he'd want to at once go to the wine cellar and attempt to find out if Amanda's message was true. No matter what fuss Aunt Clem raised he was too deeply involved to ignore what had been revealed.

Gordon walked across to Charles and said, "If you're taking a look at that cellar I'd like to join you."

Charles seemed not to care. "If you

like." He started out with everyone accompanying him except Aunt Clem and Mary Vane. The medium was still dazed. She sat there with a blank expression.

Aunt Clem was by no means so relaxed. She trailed them out to the front door protesting all the way. "I disapprove of this entire business, Charles. I *do* wish you'd listen to me!"

Her son paused before leaving to give her a resigned look and say, "Don't you recognize when you've lost, Mother?"

Aunt Clem became silent and stood with an agitated expression as they went out. Pat was ahead with Charles and Anita walked with Gordon.

She shivered. Gordon noticed and said, "Has this spooky business upset you?"

"I was on edge for awhile," she admitted. "I had no idea it would be so dramatic."

"Mary Vane is an expert," Gordon said, as they mounted the front steps of Shorecliff together in the chill darkness. "But I still can't guess what she's up to in actually confessing the murder and indicating where the remains can be found."

She paused on the verandah to stare at him in the shadows. "You're saying it was all a show."

"Wasn't it?"

"I don't know," she worried. Charles had opened the front door and they went on inside to join him and Pat.

He had been talking earnestly with Pat and now said, "I'm going straight down to the cellar. Anyone care to come along?"

"We will," Gordon said, answering for himself and Anita. "Just one thing. How can you be sure there is a body under the wine cellar floor? It may be all pure fiction made up by Mary Vane."

"I've been thinking the same thing," Anita said. "Surely it can wait until the morning."

"But why should Miss Vane lie about it?" Pat protested, half to Anita and half to Charles. "You all saw the state she was in when the seance was over."

"Much of that could be put on," Gordon said sternly.

Charles shook his head. "I'm ready to believe we've at last learned the facts. I've been devoting some days to several packets of ancient letters. And in one or two of them there were references to a well in the cellar."

"So such a well does exist," Gordon commented.

"Yes," Charles said.

"Did you discuss those letters with Mary Vane and perhaps mention the well in the cellar to her?" Gordon wanted to know.

Charles looked uneasy. "I may have," he admitted.

Gordon gave him a thoroughly scathing glance. "Then that explains it. Mary Vane just fed your own information back to you, dressed up a bit with facts she learned from some she's been reading on local history."

"I don't believe that," Charles said angrily. "Even if she learned of the existence of the cellar from me how would she know about the body being in it?"

"She's made a wild guess about that part," Gordon admitted. "And the chances are she's come up with the truth. She's not stupid."

"And I'm not as ready as you to brand her a fake," Charles declared.

Gordon shrugged. "We're all entitled to our own opinions."

"The proof will be in the cellar," Pat said. "It's getting late. If we're going down there tonight we shouldn't lose any more time."

"We'll need a lantern or two," Charles said. "The wine cellar has no electricity, and a regular flashlight won't give us enough light to work by."

"There are oil lanterns underneath the rear cellar stairs," Pat said, "we keep them handy for when the power is shut off. And you'll want tools, I suppose?"

Charles nodded. "Yes."

"There are picks and spades in the gardener's shed out back," Pat said. "I can show you the way."

"Never mind," Gordon spoke up. "I know where the shed is. I'll get what we'll need. The rest of you go down and find the lanterns. I'll join you."

Only a few minutes later they all gathered by the rear cellar stairs. The lanterns were lit and giving off a murky yellow glow. Anita was now growing as excited as the others. In spite of Gordon's skepticism she was sure they were on the brink of an overwhelming discovery.

Charles led the way along a narrow passage that went directly to the wine cellar. Anita noticed that the passage had a hard earthen floor. When they reached the wine cellar Pat held one of the smoking lanterns high while Charles fumbled with the rusty lock on the wooden door. At last he got it open and they went on into the wine cellar with its pungent smell and racks of dust-coated bottles.

Glancing around at them Charles said, "The floor here is raised and set in red brick."

Gordon stared down at the improved floor and asked, "Did you get any hint where this hidden well might be in those letters? We could dig the whole floor up and maybe not locate it."

"It's somewhere along the outside wall," Charles said. "That narrows it down so we shouldn't have too much difficulty finding it."

Anita and Pat held the lanterns while the men removed their coats and began to attack the bricks with picks. The eerie clamor of the picks on the brick floor, the flickering glow of the lanterns and the black shadows of the toiling men combined to create a weird atmosphere.

Anita noted that Pat's lovely face looked strained. And she recalled the throaty, appealing voice of Amanda that had so dominated the seance. Had it been a creation of Mary Vane's as Gordon suggested or had they listened to the true voice of the cold beauty from the other world? It was a tantalizing enigma. And because of the confusion of facts nothing would be proven in the wine cellar except that Amanda was a murderess if the body was found.

Charles had abandoned one spot and moved a few feet further on. Now his pick rang against the bricks with a wild fury.

Gordon worked a distance away at a slower pace. Between their efforts almost a third of the area along the outside wall had been dug up. They should soon know.

Anita, watching Charles slaving with the pick, noted the rivulets of sweat pouring down his temples and cheeks, worried about his frantic efforts. His unhealthy obsession with the dead Amanda could still cost them dearly. He was not sparing himself or taking his health into consideration.

"Here!" he shouted suddenly and throwing the pick aside bent down on his knees for a closer examination of the ground beneath the brick flooring. Gordon rushed to his side with his pick still in hand. "The well is directly under here," he said. And rising and retrieving his own pick he told his cousin, "Help me uncover it more."

Gordon hesitated, staring at him worriedly, the thick horn-rimmed glasses reflecting the lantern's glow in the cavern-like, shadowed wine cellar. "I guess you know what you're doing. If we find anything down here we'll have to tell the police. We could stop now."

Charles was in no mood to be argued with. "We're going ahead," he said in a near snarl. And he began to work frenziedly again.

When they had cleared a space over and around the well they shoveled away the brick and debris until at last a square plank cover with a ring of rusty iron plainly showed. With a final glance at them Charles knelt down, took hold of the ring and tugged at the plank covering. It didn't move.

Anita had the momentary sensation the air was suddenly filling with the familiar Attar of Roses perfume. The scent was as real to her as the pungent odor of dust, wine and damp had been a few minutes before. And then the rich perfume disappeared and there was only the dank smell of the cellar again. Charles gave another vicious tug on the covering and it moved.

Swinging it back he waved fiercely to Pat who was nearest him. "Bring the lantern close!"

Pat handed it to him. A hush fell over them as they stared down into the well. Charles manipulated the lantern to give them a better look. At first all that Anita could make out was that the well had gone dry long ago. And she felt sickened by the sweet smell of decay emanating from its circular, black depths.

Charles was still peering down into it.

"He's down there!" he cried out at last. "I can see bones close to the side. Look!" And he pointed. Gordon joined him in giving the well a closer inspection while she and Pat held back, having no stomach for it.

Gordon got to his feet and turned to them. "He's right," he announced in a sober voice. "There is a skeleton down there!"

It was a moment Anita would never forget. All she could think of was getting out of the stuffy cellar. Luckily the men seemed willing to leave now that the mystery had been solved. And so within a matter of minutes they were all in the hallway of Shorecliff again.

Gordon smiled cynically. "I'm going home to give Mother the happy news," he said. "I know how much she'll appreciate hearing."

Pat was full of despair. "What are you going to do next?"

"Notify the police." He looked troubled. "It can wait until the morning."

"I'll look after it for you if you like," Gordon suggested. "The State Police at Portsmouth would be best. I know some of the fellows there."

Anita recalled that he had earlier mentioned the State Police when he'd suggested she speak to them about the peculiar behavior of her husband and the events at Shorecliff. She wondered if Charles would allow his cousin to take charge of this delicate matter.

To her surprise he nodded and told Gordon, "I'd appreciate it if you would call them. Tell them I'll be here all morning."

"I'll do that," Gordon agreed. "I think we'll be less apt to get unpleasant publicity than dealing with the local police in Pennbridge." He paused to offer her a grim smile. "Goodnight, Anita. I hope all this hasn't been too much for you."

She grimaced. "I'd better feel differently in the morning."

As soon as she was alone with Charles she faced him and said, "I trust tonight's discovery frees you."

He frowned. "Frees me?"

"From Amanda," she went on seriously. "You know now that she was a murderess. You don't have to worry about defending her. You can write your story and know you have the facts."

Charles' handsome face wore a strange expression, as if he might be listening to some distant voice that was beyond her hearing. He said, "Even though she killed him she was justified."

"Is murder ever justified?" Anita asked sharply.

His tortured eyes fixed on her. "You heard what Amanda said at the seance. That he had humiliated her before her family and the town."

"And I also heard her say she'd waited for someone like you to come along," Anita warned him. "That she meant to use you."

"You're allowing yourself to get needlessly excited again," he said. "First thing you'll be having another of your spells."

"I was never ill before I came here!" she cried.

He turned wearily from her, so she could only study his lined profile. "I've heard enough complaints. I've told you that you can leave whenever you like."

"I don't want to leave you like this!" she pleaded, going to him and taking his arm. "I love you, Charles!"

He tried to free himself of her. "Then prove it by allowing me to do what I have to do."

"What she wants you to do," Anita said fiercely. "A vixen who's been dead for a hundred years and who means to live again through you. To have her story told her way in your book. An evil phantom who has tried to destroy me and is even using Pat to charm you and keep you here."

He wheeled on her angrily. "What possible connection could there be between Pat and Amanda?"

"Don't ask me to explain!" she sobbed. "I only know they are all in league against me!"

He gripped her by the arms. "Listen to me," he said. "You must stop talking this nonsense!"

"I feel so helpless here," she whimpered. "I know something dreadful will happen to you and to me. Mrs. Miller is right. Shorecliff is cursed!"

Charles still held her by the arms. "I shouldn't have allowed you to attend the seance tonight. I might have known you wouldn't understand."

"I heard Amanda speak, heard her gloat in her power over you!"

Now he surprised her by demanding, "How do you know that Gordon isn't right? That the seance and all those voices weren't merely clever tricks of Mary Vane's? Where does that leave your theory?"

"I'd still feel the same way," she told him. "I know Amanda's evil hovers over everything at Shorecliff."

"Anita, be sensible," he said. "You above all people should know what this book means to me."

"Write some other book."

"I wouldn't feel the same way about another book," he told her. "I have an inner conviction this could be my important opportunity. Don't ask me to throw it away!"

She stared at him with troubled eyes. "You still don't realize what I'm trying to explain. This impulse to carry through the book isn't yours!"

"Not mine?"

"It's Amanda's will! She made you her captive as soon as you came to Shorecliff. She's laughing at us somewhere here in the shadows! Knowing that she has brought us to this!"

Charles frowned and let her go. "You really think that? That I'm no longer making my own decisions?"

"Yes."

"I'm beginning to think you are mentally disturbed," he said in a worried voice. "I've never heard such talk from you before."

"We've never been faced with anything like this before!"

He ran a hand wearily across his forehead. "Let's not discuss it anymore to-night. We're getting nowhere. And I must be up early in the morning. The police will be coming."

"And they'll find that thing in the well," she said bitterly. "After all these years Amanda is satisfied that the body be found. She doesn't mind being remembered as a murderess anymore. Because she can count on you to weave a sad, sympathetic story that will win her an acquittal. You'll picture her as sinned against and pathetic!"

"I haven't decided just how I'll tackle the yarn," he said. "But I do feel there are things to be said in her favor."

Anita shook her head sadly. "That's Amanda speaking again. She'll always speak for you as long as you stay here."

He stared at her in silence. Then he said, "What it adds up to is you're jealous of a dead woman."

"If you want to put it that way. All right. I'll admit it."

His eyes narrowed. "Don't tell that to anyone else," he warned her. "I beg of you. They may not be as considerate as I am. It's my belief we should talk this over with Dr. Wilson."

"No!" she said in a taut voice. "I know

how that would end. Amanda would like nothing better than to tag me a lunatic."

"You must stop talking this way!"

"Only if you'll leave here and take me with you," she said. "We don't need this place or the money that goes with it! Let Pat have it! We were happy before!"

A look of understanding crossed his handsome, weary face. And he reached out and took her in his arms and held her to him. "I'm sorry, darling," he said. "I know what a strain all this has been for you. And I promise we will leave here just as soon as I can arrange it."

She pressed tightly to him. "If you only meant that!"

"I do," he insisted.

But she could tell by the way he said it he was merely humoring her. That he had decided she was on the verge of a breakdown and was trying to calm her. He had no idea of the peril he was placing them both in and no real intention of changing anything. They were hurtling to destruction under the vengeful domination of the cruel Amanda.

The police arrived shortly after nine the following morning. Anita received an introduction to Inspector Harry Decker and she liked him at once.

He was in his early forties, with dark hair, graying at the temples. His shrewd eyes and serious face revealed him as more than just an average policeman. She could understand why Gordon expressed such confidence in Decker.

After the initial talk with Charles the inspector went down to the cellar. One of his men accompanied him and carried a large canvas sack which was to be used for the remains of the young captain. After close to two hours in the old wine cellar, the policeman appeared with the sack filled and carried it out to the station wagon. A moment or so later Charles and the inspector returned.

Decker made a few notes in a small black book as he talked with Charles. "You say there is just one other member of the family living in this part of the house?"

Charles nodded. "Yes. Miss Patricia Shore. She was adopted by my Aunt Clare."

"I see. We'll have a talk with her later," the inspector said. "No need to bother her at this stage." He smiled at Anita. "Nor you, either, Mrs. Shore."

Charles seemed extremely nervous. "You don't think you'll have any difficulty proving the age of that skeleton?"

"I don't think so, Mr. Shore," Decker said affably. He might have been a successful small-town businessman in his sober blue suit and dark tie. "Merely looking at those bones tells me they weren't put down there last year or the year before."

"So it's a matter of tests and coming to a conclusion as to how long it was down there?" Charles suggested.

"Exactly." He consulted his notebook. "I think you told me there is no direct connection between this house and the adjoining one?"

"None," Charles said.

The inspector closed his book. "Well, I guess that is all for now. It's a strange affair. I'll let you know as soon as we have a lab report on those bones."

Charles seemed extremely uneasy. He said, "The story of the disappearance of that young captain and the suspicion that Amanda Shore murdered him is very well known around here."

"Indeed." Inspector Decker studied him with his shrewd gray eyes as he placed the notebook in the inside breast pocket of his blue suit. "I'm not well versed in local history. You say this was more than a century ago."

"Yes."

"And the story has come down all those years?" the inspector marveled.

"Well," Charles said, "it was a sensational affair. And then Amanda was one of those colorful characters who caught the imagination. People remembered her."

"Especially since she was believed to have murdered that poor young man," the inspector agreed dryly.

Charles was apparently not content to let it rest at that. "What I'm trying to explain is that she was a most unusual person. She was very beautiful and given to wild whims and extravagances. When she was relatively old she went to Paris and had a famous facial treatment. She returned with an enamel coating over her face that preserved its beauty in a rather strange way. She became known as the woman with the porcelain face."

Anita listened to him go on about Amanda with a sinking heart. She had no doubt the statements he uttered were Amanda's. That the evil beauty had so taken possession of his mind that he was unable to think independently any longer. She had an urge to burst out and tell the inspector what was really going on in the old mansion, of the battle she was waging to retain her husband's love. She tried to think of some way of letting the inspector know the sort of person Amanda had been. Perhaps the portrait would help. If he saw the portrait he would understand.

So she told Charles, "Why don't you take the inspector into the living room and let him see Amanda's portrait?"

Charles gave her a startled look. "I suppose I should." And to Decker, "If you'd like to see it, come along. It won't take a minute."

They stood before the portrait of the arrogant Amanda. After a moment Decker said, "It's very odd. Her eyes. They seem almost alive."

Anita nodded and asked, "Don't you find them cold, Inspector?"

Inspector Decker offered her a thoughtful smile. "I was about to remark that. There is certainly a hard gleam in them." He sighed. "Well, perhaps by this time tomorrow I can tell you about the bones."

"We'll be anxious to have your report," Charles said.

"I understand," the inspector said as they strolled slowly toward the front door. "Now I must talk with this medium, Mary Vane. After all she played an important role in the discovery of the skeleton. I must hear the story from her own lips." He smiled at Charles. "Thank you for your co-operation, Mr. Shore." And then he beamed on her. "And for your help, Mrs. Shore. I hope we may meet again."

"Yes," Anita said nervously. She could have told him that they surely would meet since she was planning to seek him out.

CHAPTER EIGHT

As soon as the inspector left Charles hurried off to the library and remained there for the rest of the morning. Anita was used to this kind of behavior and not unduly surprised. What did upset her was that Pat came down and joined him. The two remained in the library together until lunch time.

Anita went out for a stroll on the front lawn and saw the inspector's dark police car leave. She reminded herself she must drive to Portsmouth and have a talk with him at the earliest opportunity. Gordon had advised it and she would do well to listen to his advice.

Pat walked across the lawn to speak to her. The breeze ruffled Pat's hair and she stared at Anita with a shy smile. "I suppose you're wondering what I was doing closeted up with your husband all morning?"

"I did notice it," Anita said coolly, not sure what Pat was up to.

"There's a good reason for my having been there."

"That's comforting," Anita said crisply.

"I'm helping him with the notes for his book," Pat went on. "I'm typing and arranging the notes for him."

"How convenient!" she commented with open irony.

Pat's eyebrows raised. "Meaning?"

"How marvelous for Charles. I'm an excellent typist myself but he always claims my being around him makes him nervous."

Pat looked less edgy. "He told me that."

"You two have so few secrets from each other," Anita said airily. She was enraged that Charles should have asked the other girl to work with him on the book when she could have done the job equally well. It was another of his attempts to widen the break between them and at the same time give him an excuse for spending his days with Pat.

Pat's mouth took on a crooked smile. "You hate me almost as much as you do Amanda," she accused her.

"Perhaps I do," Anita readily admitted. "And for the same reasons."

Pat laughed scornfully. "Charles told me. You're jealous of poor dead Amanda. You think she's trying to steal him from you."

Anita lifted her chin defiantly. "That may not be as fantastic as you think."

"It's priceless!" Pat laughed. "Just priceless! Imagine having a hang-up about a century dead rival!"

"If you're seriously working on that book you may come to believe some of the things I do," Anita told her. "You were at the seance last night. You heard Amanda say she had been waiting for Charles to come."

"That!" Pat said disgustedly. "That was Mary Vane putting on an act. She was making it up from things she'd learned from Charles. Saying the body was in the cellar was a guess on her part and a good one. She just put two and two together once she found out about the hidden well."

"Perhaps you're right," Anita said. "But the voice was no more hers than was that of the child's."

"I'd put Mary Vane down as an accomplished actress," Pat said. "And you can bet she'll make last night pay. When the story gets out she was responsible for finding that skeleton all the believers in spiritualism will be lining up for her meetings."

"Perhaps," Anita said. "Personally I think there was a warning as well as a message in that seance. The warning was clearly that Amanda expects to take full control of Charles until she has him write the book in a fashion sympathetic to her. Then her spirit may come to rest."

Pat gave her a disdainful look. "No wonder Charles is worried about you losing your mind."

"He needn't concern himself on that score," Anita told her, "especially when his own problem is so much more urgent."

"I don't care what you say or do," Pat said defiantly. "I'm going on working with him."

"I expected that," Anita told her.

The pretty brown-haired girl smiled coldly again. "Just so long as you aren't surprised!" And with complete self-confidence she wheeled around and strode back to the house.

Anita stared after her bleakly. Each day life at Shorecliff was getting more difficult for her. From the very beginning there had been an unspoken feud between her and Pat, who resented Anita and Charles for taking the house and most of the money away from her. Apparently deciding she might be able to win Charles for herself she was now coming out into the open with her play for him.

Once again Anita suspected that the other girl might be the phantom with the porcelain face as well. It was the type of audacious scheme in which Pat would revel. And the role of the ghost offered ample cover for the malicious attacks made on her life. It was possible Pat might be her most dangerous enemy. It was something she must talk over again with Gordon. The mere thought of him relaxed her. At least she could count on Gordon.

It was after lunch and she was sitting in the living room with a magazine on her lap when the doorbell rang. Mrs. Miller appeared quickly to answer it and she heard Mary Vane asking for Charles.

"Mr. Shore is in the library and he's asked not to be disturbed," the old housekeeper said crossly.

"It's urgent that I talk with him," Mary Vane maintained in her hollow voice.

Anita went out to the hall. She told Mrs. Miller, "I'll take care of this." The old woman scowled and went back down the corridor.

"I'm here to see *Mr.* Shore."

"I heard you," she assured her, giving her a measuring glance. The dark woman's gauntly attractive face was pale; she could tell the medium was in an agitated state. "Mr. Shore is working. He doesn't like to be disturbed. He's starting his book."

"But I can help him!" Mary Vane insisted.

Anita smiled bleakly. "He already has help. Miss Shore is doing his typing."

"I can do more than typing," Mary Vane said importantly. "I can keep him in touch with Amanda."

"You really believe that?"

The dark woman looked offended. "How can you question that? You were at the seance last night. You must have heard Amanda speak."

"I heard someone speak," Anita said carefully.

"I've suffered for my dedication to my work," the upset woman said. "I've been asked to leave Mrs. Morehouse's home at once because of my truthfulness last night."

"I was afraid it might get you into trouble."

"When the inspector came to question me that finished it," Mary Vane said grimly. "But I have demonstrated my psychic powers. I should be allowed to remain here until I have penetrated all the dark places and brought truth to this house."

"The only one who can give you permission to stay in Shorecliff is my husband," Anita told her. "And if you wish to see him I would advise that you return later."

"When?"

"Before dinner would be a good time."

Mary Vane's gaunt face showed a shadow of worry. "I guess I can force the old woman to let me stay until then. She's in quite a state."

"I can imagine," Anita said quickly. And then with a glance down the corridor in the direction of the closed door of the library, she turned to the medium again, and said, "I'll be frank, Miss Vane. I'd prefer you didn't try to talk my husband into keeping you here."

"Why do you say that?" she asked, almost angrily.

"Because you create an unhealthy atmosphere. I'm worried about him as it is. I think this Amanda Shore affair is destroying his mind."

"If I stay I'll be a help to him."

"Conjuring up Amanda again? Giving him weird messages? You've had some success here. Why don't you leave when you're doing well."

"I'd rather discuss that with Mr. Shore," the medium said firmly.

186

"I know," Anita said. "And I can predict what his reaction will be. He'll arrange for you to stay on in this part of the house."

"That's what I want," the medium said.

"But it's not healthy for him," she warned.

"I'd let him make up his mind about that," Mary Vane said as she turned to go.

She returned at six o'clock as Anita had suggested. Anita didn't hear the conversation between the medium and her husband. But the outcome was exactly what she'd predicted. Charles offered Mary Vane accommodation and engaged her services for a series of seances.

When she questioned Charles as to the wisdom of this he looked at her with astonishment, "But Miss Vane gave us our first important clue to the mystery. But for her I'd never have discovered the skeleton."

"I'm sure you would have if you'd given the matter some thought," Anita disagreed. "You were the one who supplied her with information about the well in the cellar."

"But she brought it all into focus," he argued. "I've made up my mind. Miss Vale is remaining here."

Anita could only see it as another reverse. Since Mary Vane knew she was an unwelcome guest as far as Anita was concerned it would cause extra tension in an atmosphere well supplied with it. Pat was behaving in a brazen way with Charles and was hardly civil to her. Charles continued to look more harried each day and to grow more obviously nervous. Even Mrs. Miller was infected with the tension and became more difficult.

That evening around dusk Anita received a phone call from Gordon. His first comment was, "I understand you have a new house guest."

"The same one you lost," she told him.

"Mother is furious," he said. "She's sure the murder story is going to be given headlines and she blames Mary Vane for bringing it about."

"She should only share part of the blame," Anita said.

"I agree," Gordon said. "Are you alone?"

"Technically no. But I might as well be. Mary Vane is upstairs in her room and Pat and Charles are working in the library."

"Cozy!"

"Very," she said with irony.

"In that case you can slip out and meet me on the lawn. I have some things I want to talk to you about I can't discuss over the phone."

"I'm slightly allergic to lawns," Anita reminded him. "Especially since the other night when I had that frightening meeting with the phantom."

"You needn't worry tonight," Gordon promised. "I'll stay with you every second."

"Sounds better," she said.

"I'll leave now," he told her. "You do the same."

She slipped on a sweater and hurried down the verandah steps. Gordon was waiting for her on the gravel path.

He smiled. "You managed it. No one noticed."

"No one pays the slightest attention to me anymore."

"Not even Charles?"

"No."

"He's a fool then. And I'd like to tell him so." They began to walk slowly toward the cliff. "If I were your husband you'd never get out from under my watchful eye."

She gave a small laugh. "That sounds almost as bad as my present plight."

"I didn't mean it to," he said in a serious tone. "I wondered about you all day."

"Thanks," she said. "I thought about you several times."

"Call me whenever you like," he urged. "If anything frightens you always remember I can be reached at the shop."

"I know. It's one of the things that makes it possible for me to stay on here," she said, "knowing I can count on you and that you're never too far away."

"Mother's in one of her bad moods," he said with a sigh. "She's locked herself in her room. Won't speak to anyone — not even me since I reminded her she was the one who brought Mary Vane down here."

"Is she still upset about possible bad newspaper publicity?"

"Yes."

They had come to the edge of the cliff and it was now completely dark, without a moon or stars. Far out across the bay a buoy rang and a red light showed in the night. At the end of the cape the beam of a lighthouse cut the blackness in a wide swath with monotonous regularity. Below the waves had a melancholy sound as the tide was low and the water retreated.

"I think she's worrying about nothing," Anita told Gordon. "Even if the press does feature the story how can something that happened over a century ago hurt the family today?"

"I agree with you," he replied unhappily. "But you can't make Mother see anything. If she makes up her mind that's it. And she's made up her mind."

"I'm sorry for her and you."

"She enjoys being miserable," Gordon said. "And I'm used to it." Changing the subject he asked, "Did Inspector Decker come down himself with the police car?"

"Yes. A car and station wagon came. They took what they found at the bottom of the well away in a canvas bag." She shuddered and stared at the distant beam of the lighthouse. "I can't imagine ever going down into that cellar again."

"It was a horrible experience," he said. "Yet I don't think it touched Charles. He's worked himself up into such a state. Did you watch him closely last night?"

"Yes," she said. "I tried to reason with him afterward. It was no use."

"Do you know what I think?" Gordon drew out his words significantly.

"What?"

"I believe he's had some kind of relapse from this accident. It seems to me he's teetering on the very edge of insanity."

She turned away, her back to the young man. She was ashamed to have him get even a faint glimpse of her tormented face in the darkness. Trying to control the tremor in her voice, she said, "I'm coming around to the same belief."

"Yet you remain here?"

"I can't desert him. Not now! Not let Amanda destroy him!"

"You're a brave girl," Gordon said quietly. "Braver than he deserves."

She turned impulsively. "It has to be better! It has to be!"

"Until we're more certain of that," Gordon said meaningfully, "I have something for you." He reached in his side jacket pocket. "Take this."

She stared down at the weapon. It was a small, ugly-looking gun with a squat barrel. She drew back. "I couldn't take it! I've never used a gun!"

"This one is simple. There's a safety lock. I'll show you how to release it. Then you just point it and pull the trigger."

"Unless you agree to take this weapon I'm going to the police myself," Gordon said. "I won't have you here without at least something to defend yourself."

"I can always phone you."

"And what could happen between the time you called and I got here? You could be murdered a dozen times! Take the gun!"

"My chief enemy is Amanda," she protested. "What use are bullets against a ghost?"

"I'm thinking more in terms of Charles," Gordon said grimly. "You must take this weapon."

In the end she agreed and he showed her how to use it. She was revolted by the hard, metallic feel of the weapon through the pocket of her sweater. With each step she took, it moved against her body, telling her it was there and ready to kill. She'd accepted it only to placate Gordon as he was so plainly worried about her safety. But she had no intention of continually carrying the weapon as he'd urged. Instead she planned to hide it somewhere in her room where she could get at it in case of a sudden threat.

Gordon saw her to the door. "Remember," he warned her, "don't tell anyone about the gun. Not anyone!"

"I have no one to confide in except you," she said. And touched by his concern she leaned close and touched her lips gently to his cheek. "Thanks, Gordon."

An eerie stillness had settled over the dimly lighted old mansion. She imagined that Charles and Pat were still down in the library working. She quickly made her way up to the bedroom and as soon as she'd shut the door behind her she began to think about hiding the gun. After a quick survey of the room she went to the big clothes closet. It had a high shelf with some hat boxes on it.

She stood on a plain chair and carefully deposited the gun in the largest of the hat boxes. She could be certain that no one would ever bother it there. And if she ever should need it she knew where it was and could easily get it in a hurry. Relieved, she put the chair back and prepared for bed.

It would have been unthinkable if anyone had suggested a few weeks ago she might be hiding a weapon to protect herself against Charles. She would have indignantly denied it. And yet she had just done this very thing. Perhaps Gordon was too much of an alarmist, but she had also been shocked by the change in Charles and the haggard look that continually marred his handsome face.

She was in bed when Charles came up. She heard him call goodnight to Pat. And when he came into the room she closed her eyes and pretended to be asleep. He didn't challenge her play-acting and within a few minutes he turned out the light and got into bed at her side. She lay there scarcely daring to breathe until she heard him begin to snore softly. Then she relaxed and fell asleep herself.

She opened her eyes to the darkness and instinctively felt that Charles was no longer beside her. The bedclothes were turned back and the bed was empty! Nor was there any light from the bathroom. Her eyes darted back and forth in darkness around her; her brooding fear became a live choking thing once more. She was certain she heard a movement in the corner of the room and raised herself up a little.

Then with terrifying speed the figure materialized. All she could see plainly was the familiar expressionless face of Amanda. The fragrance of Attar of Roses filled the air and the pink porcelain features of Amanda hovered just above her. She saw the phantom's arm raise and then come down on her. And again she felt the sting of pain in her arm. Between shock and pain she fainted.

She came awake to a tableau similar to one she had experienced before. A grave-faced Dr. Wilson flanked her bed. Charles was at his side. Near the foot of the bed stood Pat.

Dr. Wilson shook his head. "The old story, Mrs. Shore. Convulsions and blackout. Why haven't you come to my office as I asked?"

"I didn't need to," she said weakly. "I wasn't ill."

"That's not so, Doctor," Charles protested. "And Pat will bear me out in this. My wife has been in a most troubled state. She's talked wildly ever since the night of that first attack."

"What do you say to that?" Dr. Wilson asked her.

"I deny it."

"You can't deny you were ill when I came here tonight. You were actually in the middle of a convulsion. It took some time to bring you out of it."

Anita stared up at him with naked animal fear in her eyes. "She came again!"

"Mrs. Shore!" he reproved.

"It was Amanda!" she persisted. "She came and did something to me again. It was the same as last time."

Charles gave the doctor a despairing look and raised a hand. "You hear her, Doctor. This is typical of what has been going on."

Dr. Wilson's thin face showed concern. "You've either got to rid your mind of these fantasies, Mrs. Shore, or we'll have to send you to a hospital right away."

She sensed that he meant this and experienced a new fear — the terror of a public or even a private mental hospital. Charles might be delighted to lock her away.

"I'm sorry," she said. "I'm nearly always confused when I come out of these spells."

"Much better," Dr. Wilson said approvingly.

"I didn't mean to be such a bother," she went on playing a game with the sedate doctor.

"No need to apologize," he said in an expansive tone. "It's my job to take care of your health. Still, these attacks do puzzle me. I keep thinking of epilepsy. Yet you say you have no history of the disease in your family."

"I don't think so," she said. "I'm not sure."

"The proper place for an examination is my office," he said. "And I'll expect you to show yourself there within a few days."

"Yes, Doctor." She was determined not to argue with him. She had to win time. "Tonight's attack wasn't so bad. I feel much better already."

"It was minor compared to the other one," he agreed. "Still I'll feel a lot easier when I know what's causing them."

"Thank you, Doctor," she said.

"I've left some sedative," he told her. "Take a dose and get some rest."

Pat remained in the room with her after the two men had gone out. She looked strikingly beautiful even in the middle of the night, Anita forlornly concluded as she gazed up at the brown-haired girl in her green chiffon dressing gown.

Pat eyed her cynically. "You changed your tune quick."

"Why do you say that?"

"I heard what you said about Amanda attacking you," Pat went on. "And when the doctor hinted about an asylum you reversed yourself completely."

"I was confused. I didn't know what I was saying at first."

Pat smiled with meaning. "You should be delighted. You fooled the doctor without any trouble. But you didn't fool me. You're sure you saw Amanda and she was responsible for your attack."

Anita stared up at her. "You wanted me to go on saying that," she told her. "You and Charles would like nothing better than to have me locked up in some mental hospital."

"That's where anyone who talks about seeing phantoms should be," Pat said hotly.

"I'll remember that," she said wryly. "Since you may begin talking about them yourself, one day."

"No thanks," Pat said sarcastically. "I'll leave Amanda to you. I'm satisfied with Charles!" And she swept out of the room.

Charles returned a short while later in a sober frame of mind. He asked Anita if she were feeling better and when she assured him she was he went about mixing the dose of sedative.

As Anita drank it, he said, "I think the doctor is right. You need more medical attention at once."

"I'll see him," she promised.

Charles frowned at her. "I'm not sure he is competent to deal with your illness. I'm thinking more in the terms of Boston and a specialist."

She handed him the empty glass and shook her head. "No, Charles. I'm not leaving Shorecliff under any circumstances."

He took the glass, and with a sigh, turned and went to the bathroom with it. In a moment the lights were turned out again and thanks to the sedative she fell asleep almost at once. Her last thoughts were of Charles and the disappointed look on his face when she'd refused to leave. Amanda had taken possession of every part of him. He was thinking her thoughts alone.

She went down to breakfast the following morning in spite of Charles' protests. While having her morning shower she noticed the tiny blue bruise on her upper left arm. And this confirmed her belief that the phantom Amanda had wielded some weird weapon against her. Whatever had been plunged into her arm had caused this convulsion.

It was another sunny morning and after breakfast she lingered downstairs. She was standing on the verandah when Mary Vane joined her.

"So you had a seizure last night, Mrs. Shore," she said with a hint of sarcasm.

"A slight illness. It was nothing," Anita said.

The medium shook her head. "Don't try to fool me, Mrs. Shore. I know better. You would be wise to avoid offending the spirits."

"What are you saying?" she asked, looking into the medium's deep-set, black eyes and seeing only hatred there.

"Amanda was in the house last night," Mary Vane continued. "I know. And it was Amanda who avenged herself on you for the abuse you've been heaping on her."

"You're insane!" Anita said angrily.

A smile, not a pleasant one, crossed the medium's gaunt face. "You don't really think that, Mrs. Shore. And you know what I'm talking about." And she left Anita standing there and went back inside.

Anita was stunned by the woman's boldness. And she was terrified by the mounting hatred of her in the old mansion. She realized Gordon had been right. It was time she spoke to the authorities about what was going on and asked their advice. Inspector Harry Decker had seemed a pleasant, shrewd man. She would take her problems to him.

She waited until she was sure Charles and Pat were at work in the library. Then she went out, got into the sports car and quietly drove out toward the main road. She didn't feel safe until she was several miles from Shorecliff. Then she took the road to Portsmouth.

She reached the busy little city in mid-morning and parked her car in front of State Police Headquarters. Inspector Decker, a desk-sergeant told her, was in court and would not return to his office for a half-hour. She elected to wait for him.

The time passed slowly. She tried to read a magazine but couldn't calm her nerves enough to concentrate. At last, when she'd almost reached the limit of her endurance a young policeman came and took her to Inspector Decker's private office.

The gray-haired inspector rose to greet her with a smile. "Strange you should arrive at this moment," he said. "I was just about to phone your husband. We have an interesting report on that skeleton."

CHAPTER NINE

The inspector's statement aroused Anita's curiosity. She said, "You haven't lost much time in your investigation."

"We tried to rush this," he said with one of his shrewd glances. "It's really a very strange affair."

"I agree," she said quietly.

"Please sit down, Mrs. Shore." And when she'd taken a seat in the rather shabby leather chair available to her he settled himself behind his desk. "The lab claims the bones must be at least a century old."

"Then that settles it," she said.

He nodded. "It would seem to indicate the legend of Amanda Shore murdering the man who spurned her is true."

"My husband will be extremely interested," she said.

Inspector Harry Decker smiled wisely. "I'm sure of that. But I'm not so positive his aunt will be delighted. She wanted me to forget the entire business."

"I know," Anita said. "She has an exaggerated feeling about the family. She's afraid the revelation of the murder will hurt the Shore name."

"I understand that," the inspector said. "But it seems much ado about nothing. It will cause a small flurry of interest and make a good newspaper story. But it is all of the past."

"I suppose," Anita agreed wryly. "Although sometimes I wonder."

The man behind the desk registered mild surprise. "Your statement interests me, Mrs. Shore. But then I suppose you have come to see me for a particular reason."

"I have."

He lifted a paper from his desk and studied it casually. "I think I'd better phone your husband and give him the details of the lab investigation personally. There are some technical details to be mentioned and it would seem preferable to your acting as my messenger."

"I'm certain it would," she said.

Putting the paper aside he focused his full attention on her again. "Now just what is your problem, Mrs. Shore?"

She hesitated. Now that it came to

telling him her story she was afraid she would be met with ridicule. The drab, official atmosphere of the small office was little suited to such a confession. And no one knew better than herself how few people believed in ghosts.

Searching for a proper start, she said, "Did the atmosphere of Shorecliff strike you as somewhat unusual?"

He rubbed his chin with his left hand for a few seconds. "Now that you mention it, I suppose it did."

"I was sure you must have felt it," she said, gaining assurance.

"Everyone seemed more worried about events that happened over a hundred years ago than what is going on there now," he ruminated. "That is pretty strange."

"Very strange," she agreed.

He eyed her thoughtfully. "I received the impression your family is a pretty neurotic lot. Including your husband. I haven't had the opportunity of meeting him before. I know few families in Pennbridge."

"But you have met Gordon Morehouse?"

He smiled in recognition of the name. "Gordon is over this way pretty often. He is a friend of a fellow I know who has an antique shop here. You know anything about antiques, Mrs. Shore?"

"Not much."

"You should! I promise you that," the inspector said earnestly. "This friend of mine has made a comfortable living for years just buying and selling old pieces of furniture and the like. I wish I'd had the sense to find something like that instead of going in for police work."

She was surprised. "Don't you enjoy your work?"

"Sometimes," he said. "Only sometimes, Mrs. Shore. But we've digressed. We were about to consider your problem."

"Yes," she said, awkwardly. She stared down at her hands. "I'm only afraid you're going to find what I have to say hard to believe."

He leaned back in his chair. "I can't offer an opinion until I hear what your story is. I've heard some strange ones in this office. So don't feel you are unique or apt to surprise me."

She raised her eyes to him gratefully. "Thank you. I will get on with it. I don't want to waste your time."

"Don't worry about that."

"Very weird things have happened to me since I came to live at Shorecliff," she said.

"Weird things?" he questioned.

"I have been the victim of a number of violent attacks." She paused. "And the attacks were made on me by the ghost of Amanda Shore."

He showed no expression. When he spoke, his tone was mild and controlled. "Why do you say that, Mrs. Shore?"

She licked her lips nervously. Her throat had become tight, her mouth felt parched. "Because I have seen her — seen a phantom with a dreadful-looking porcelain face. A face like a death mask!"

"Where have you seen this ghost?"

And now she began to detail the attacks and told him the entire story, ending with an account of the ghost coming to her in her bed and stabbing her with the hat pin a second time. She concluded, "When I came around Dr. Wilson and my husband were standing by the bed. They both took it for granted I'd had another spell. Neither of them would listen to my story about the ghost."

"I see," the inspector said dryly.

She gave him an appealing look. "Will you please believe I'm telling the truth? It may be a ghost or someone posing as one. But I saw something."

The inspector's shrewd eyes were measuring her. "I like that last, Mrs. Shore," he said. "You saw something. Now there is a comment I can safely put down in my report. I can hardly state you were chased by a porcelain-faced spirit."

"But if you're going to help me shouldn't you consider all possibilities?" she said. "And I feel it could very well be a ghost."

Now he bent forward and leaned his arms on the desk, as he enquired, "Can you give me any motive for a woman dead a hundred years to attack you?"

"Yes," she said solemnly. "I believe that Amanda is in love with my husband. And in her ghostly way she plans to make use of him to bring her to life again."

The inspector sighed. "I'll ask you to amplify that statement, Mrs. Shore. How can he bring her back to life again?"

"In his book." She despaired that he would understand her. "Amanda wants posterity to remember her as a noble woman who murdered only because her proud spirit was bitterly wounded. She is hypnotizing my husband so he will portray her that way."

"How is she hypnotizing him?" Decker asked patiently.

"Don't ask me that," she said, becoming more miserable and unsure of herself every minute under his wilting stare. "I only know he has changed since he's lived at Shorecliff. He's not at all like the man I married. First I worried that it might be the result of his accident."

"He had an accident?"

"Yes," she said. And she had to explain about the car crash and his head injuries.

"Head injuries, eh?" he considered.

"I'm not sure that Charles is responsible any longer."

"A lot of your conclusions are pretty melodramatic, Mrs. Shore," Harry Decker warned her.

"I realize that."

"And about those seizures of your own," he said. "The convulsive fits."

"The phantom caused them," she said, tautly. "Amanda stabbed me with something."

The inspector sighed, drew back his chair and got up. He moved around the table to stand staring at her. And she was somewhat relieved to see that his stern face wore a rather sympathetic look.

"I don't know what to advise you, Mrs. Shore," he said at last.

"I had to talk to someone."

He raised a hand and dropped it to his thigh in resignation. "Of course you did," he said wearily. He frowned at her. "If all you've told me is true it would appear that even I have underestimated the confusion at Shorecliff."

"It is not a happy house," she said. "Now I'm afraid for my life."

"I gather that," he said mildly. "And yet I doubt if the danger is as great as you think."

She gave him a pleading look. "Can't you help in some way?"

"I very much want to," he assured her. "It's just that it's not easy."

"I can't go on much longer."

"One of the first things I'd like to do is sound out Dr. Wilson," the inspector said. "I'd like to get his views on what is going on in that old house. And I want to hear his medical definition of your case."

"But Charles has him wrapped around his finger," Anita protested. "He'll say exactly what Charles has put in his mind. And that is the opinion that Amanda has forced on Charles with her spell."

"I'm sorry, Mrs. Shore. But I'll have to go at this my way."

"They'll delude you."

"I'm not easily fooled," Decker assured her. "And if I am in the beginning, I usually come to my senses in time." He paused. "Where will I be with your wild story if Dr. Wilson tells me it is you, not your husband, who has the sick mind?"

"I'll take any test. Try me with anything!"

"We can go into that later. Just now I'd like you to go back to Shorecliff and try and calm yourself. Act as if nothing had happened."

"But I'm afraid I'll be killed!"

"I'm going to talk to your husband on the phone," the inspector promised. "And I'll make it clear to him that any further violence at Shorecliff would bring him under suspicion. That should help guarantee your safety."

"You won't tell him I've been here to see you?" she asked nervously.

"Not if you don't want me to."

"I don't." She knew that he was treating her like a person with delusions. And she had a strong fear that after a chat with Dr. Wilson he would be certain of this.

Inspector Decker rubbed the back of his neck uneasily. "I'll do all I can for you, Mrs. Shore. But I don't think there is a lot to be done. This danger you mention could be mostly in your mind induced by the undoubtedly gloomy atmosphere of that old house."

She knew the interview was over so she got up. "Thank you, Inspector."

He saw her to the door. "I'll keep all you've told me in mind."

"Yes," she said, quietly, not wanting to look in those shrewd eyes again.

Decker apparently sensed her depressed mood. "You mustn't consider yourself friendless and alone," he pointed out. "You say that Gordon Morehouse is doing all he can to help you. And there is his mother. And I'm sure this Patricia is not the sort to pretend to be a phantom and harm you. Just try to take it easy, Mrs. Shore."

"I'll try," she murmured. She had told him about everything except the gun and she had a brief impulse to mention it but then decided against it.

"Your husband may not be as mentally distressed as you think," he said. "It may well be that after I've gotten in touch with him and told him about the age of the skeleton he will be in a completely different mood."

"I doubt it," she said.

"Don't be too sure," he reasoned with her. "He may be seriously concerned that the skeleton is of more recent vintage. That the murder might be a recent one. When he discovers the victim was the young man Amanda murdered he's bound to feel easier."

"He was upset before the discovery of the skeleton," she said. "And Mary Vane will use all her trickery to keep him in a state."

"If she has been practicing as a professional medium in Boston the police there will have a report on her. I'll check and see what I can find. Something helpful may turn up."

"I hope so," she said fervently.

"By the time you reach Shorecliff your husband will have heard the news," Decker assured her. "I'll come by one of these days. In the meanwhile if you are seriously upset you know where to reach me."

"Thanks," she said.

She left feeling completely discouraged. She hadn't made any progress with the inspector. He regarded her as a female crackpot unduly influenced by the ghostly atmosphere at Shorecliff. But she knew there was more to it than that, yet she'd been unable to present a convincing story to him.

Probably she'd been wrong to mention ghosts at all. Certainly the fact she'd had the two attacks and a doctor had been called in didn't put her in any better light.

And if the mild, fair-minded inspector was skeptical of all she'd said she could hardly hope for anyone else to understand that Amanda's evil spirit was directing all the spiteful activity. Because he lived at Shore-cliff and was one of the family, Gordon was one of the few who knew what she was talking about.

So it wasn't strange that she should drive directly to his antique barn.

She was luckier in finding him this time. He was in the main showroom polishing a beautiful old grandfather's clock. He was wearing the same leather apron as on that other day and paused in his work when he heard her come in.

"Welcome, Anita," he smiled. "You're just in time to see this beauty before we ship it to Boston."

She tried to throw off her gloom and show some interest in the antique that meant so much to him. "Is it very old?" she asked.

His hand fondled the tall clock affection-ately. "It was built in 1809. Made by two German-Swiss clock makers. One did the woodwork and the other fashioned the mechanism. This is their masterpiece."

"You've polished it splendidly," Anita marvelled.

"There are at least three hundred and sixty-five different kinds of wood in it," Gordon said. "And perhaps between twenty and thirty thousand pieces of inlay."

"A piece of wood for every day in the year," she said.

"That was the idea." He studied it fondly. "You can see that the clock is basically made of mahogany. But there are many imported woods in it also. Even bits of ivory and ebony."

"How has it been kept so well over the years?"

Gordon laughed. "I found it in a Vermont farmhouse. It wasn't working and they were using it as a storage place for eggs. It had been knocked over and banged and bruised. But I've managed to restore it as you see it here."

"I don't blame you for feeling proud!" she exclaimed.

He nodded. "It's like my own creation now." He turned away from the clock to study her. "You're not looking too well. I heard you were ill again last night. Shouldn't you have stayed quiet today?"

"No," she shook her head as they stood there in the gloom and silence of the antique-filled barn. "I've been to the police."

"The police?" he lifted his eyebrows.

"You suggested that I should."

"I thought it might be wise," he agreed with some caution. "Who did you talk to?"

"Inspector Decker in Portsmouth. The one who came to the house yesterday. He's the one you said I should see."

"That's right," Gordon said. "I know him fairly well."

"He mentioned that."

"How did you make out?"

She sighed. "I'm afraid I didn't make out at all."

Gordon's handsome young face showed concern. His eyes searched her face. "You told him all that had gone on?"

"Yes. But the inspector apparently doesn't believe in ghosts. Nor the evil a malevolent spirit can work from that other world."

"I guess maybe he has enough trouble to cope with on this side of the spirit world," he suggested.

"That's about what he told me," she said bitterly. "I'm sure I wound up making him think I'm the psychotic."

"That's too bad, Anita," the young man said sincerely. "I'm going in to Portsmouth before I go home. I'll try and see him and have a talk with him."

Gordon's words gave her new hope. She looked at him eagerly. "Would you?"

"You know I'll do anything I can for you," he said.

"If I didn't know that I wouldn't go back to Shorecliff now!"

The young antique dealer sighed. "It might be better if you didn't! Shorecliff is moldy with the past. We're all dominated by the dead ones there. I can tell you Mother is in some rage over that seance and the body being found. She put Mary Vane out. And the crazy part of it is that Mother will be dead herself within a few years at most!"

"Before I left today Mary came to me and ranted wildly about Amanda having been in the house last night, telling me she knew that it was Amanda who had brought on my spell," Anita said.

Gordon looked angry. "Perhaps she does know more than we give her credit for."

"I'm beginning to think the same thing," Anita said. "After all she has been in the house ever since the visitations began. And who would know better than she how to pretend to be a ghost — and make those vicious attacks on me?"

"It fits."

"Only one thing puzzles me," Anita went

on. "In the beginning she was in your section of the house. And you say there is no direct connection between the two houses. So it would have been impossible for her to make her way to my bedroom."

"She mightn't have gone directly from one house to another," Gordon suggested. "It's possible she went outdoors and found some door unlocked in your section and made her way in through it."

"I hadn't thought of that," she admitted. "It would mean exposing herself to possible discovery. A lot of people in both houses would have more chance of seeing her that way."

"If she was desperate enough she'd try it," Gordon said. "But then you still think you may be dealing with the real Amanda. A true phantom."

"That's so," she said. "Inspector Decker is going to contact Boston and try and find out something more about Mary Vane. According to him the police have a file on all professional mediums."

"Sounds as if it might be helpful," Gordon said. "You may have done better with the inspector than you guess."

"Let's hope so," she said. "And you will talk to him as well?"

"Depend on it," he said.

"I'd better be getting back," she said. "Charles will be in a rage if he finds me gone."

"Did the inspector have anything to say about the skeleton?" Gordon wanted to know as he saw her to the door of the shop.

She grimaced. "How could I forget to mention that! Of course, he had news about it! The lab report shows that it is really old. He accepts that it dates back to Amanda's time."

"So!" Gordon said. "That settles that. Mary Vane's guess was a good one — if it was a guess."

"Remember the information was given to us in Amanda's voice," Anita said with a tiny shiver. "The voice seemed exactly right. It makes me nervous just to recall it."

"Mary Vane probably has a repertoire of voices," he said with a grim smile. "Don't take it too seriously."

"I don't know," she said. "I honestly don't know what to think."

She left him on this note. It was exactly the way she felt. She had seen the police and told her story. If Gordon was able to convince the skeptical police official there was more truth than fantasy in her story it might help. She could only trust that it would.

When she returned to Shorecliff, she found, to her surprise, a strange car with a Massachusetts license plate parked in front of the verandah. When she entered the house Mrs. Miller came to meet her.

"You have a visitor," she said. "She's waiting in the living room."

Anita thanked her and walked into the living room. Doris Benson, an old friend, was there waiting.

"Doris! I had no idea you were coming!" she exclaimed.

Doris, a plain girl with a neat figure and a good smile, stood up and embraced Anita. "I'm on vacation and I knew you had come to Pennbridge to live. I thought I'd stop by to say hello."

"You'll do more than that. I insist you stay overnight at least!"

"I don't know," Doris hesitated. "I planned to drive on to Maine."

"It can wait until tomorrow," Anita insisted. "We have so much to talk about. I haven't seen you since the wedding." Doris had worked in the same office and was perhaps her closest friend.

So it was settled and Doris brought her

bag in from the car. Mrs. Miller found her a room not far from Charles and Anita's room. While Doris was unpacking they had their first chance to talk. Anita sat on the bed while Doris plodded between her open suitcase and the dresser. When she finished she gave Anita a sharp look.

"You don't look nearly as well as at the wedding," she said. "Have you been ill?"

Even though Doris was a good friend Anita hesitated to tell her everything that had gone on. She shrugged. "Sort of."

"Sort of?" Doris said cynically. She studied Anita with some concern. "What kind of an answer is that?"

"I've had two spells since we came down here," Anita said awkwardly. She knew her friend too well to think she'd be easy to deceive. "Convulsions and blackouts."

"Convulsions!" Doris said. "I don't believe it!"

She nodded. "It's true."

Doris looked startled. "But you never had any kind of illness before you were married," she said. "You were the healthiest girl in the office."

She smiled wryly. "Times have changed."

"I guess so," Doris said, a grim look on her plain face. She glanced around the rather drab bedroom. "This room is just as

221

gloomy as the rest of the house. I don't know how you stand it. Probably that's what's making you ill."

"There's a little more to it," she said.

"I think it's time we had a straight talk," Doris suggested.

And so Anita told her everything that had happened. Her friend sat by her with an expression that grew constantly more incredulous. And when Anita had finally finished there was long silence before Doris commented:

"It's the most fantastic story I've ever heard. If anyone else told it to me I'd say they were crazy!"

"I'm afraid that's the general reaction," she sighed.

Doris looked at her. "But I know you. And if you say these things are so I won't argue."

"Thanks."

"This Patricia is a minor problem," her friend went on. "A pretty girl on the make for your husband . . . you'll have to get used to that and learn how to deal with her."

"Unless she also happens to be playing the phantom role and trying to murder me," Anita reminded her.

"I'd like to rule her out as a suspect,"

Doris said. "But I suppose we can't."

"My own theory right now is that Mary Vane is the culprit," Anita said. "But proving it is another thing."

"The part that upsets me most is the way Charles has let you down," Doris complained. "I don't mind telling you I was jealous of you at the wedding. I thought you were getting the perfect husband — if there is such a creature."

"I thought so, too," Anita agreed. "And we were so happy in Boston."

"I'm sure of that."

"The trouble began as soon as he entered this house."

"That's an awfully strong argument for the existence of some evil spirit as you've suggested. Otherwise, why would he change?" Doris went on.

"I don't know," she said unhappily. "The idea of the book seems to dominate him. And of course the book is Amanda."

"I've never had much time for spiritualism and all that stuff," Doris admitted. "But when you run up against something like this it makes you wonder."

"I've done an awful lot of wondering," she said. "And sometimes I think that Amanda is going to win out. I'm so glad you came and I've been able to talk to you.

The only other person I've had to count on is Gordon."

"The fellow next door," Doris said. "Sounds nice."

"I want you to meet him."

Doris gave her a warning smile. "No matchmaking. I'm not interested in trying my luck in this ghost-ridden palace."

Anita gave her a pitiful smile back. "Oh, Doris, it's so good to have you here! It's like airing out this old house. What's going to happen to me?"

"If this ghost keeps visiting you and you continue having those spells it's likely your husband will place you in some quiet private hospital."

"I'm terrified that could happen," Anita admitted.

"I think this Gordon gave you good advice and you were right in going to the police. Perhaps the inspector will find a way to help you."

Anita stood up quickly. "I have no right to burden you with my worries," she said. "You're here on a holiday. I'll leave you to have a shower in peace and change. Then I want you to meet Charles and the others."

Doris rolled her eyes. "I don't know whether I trust myself to see him. I'm liable to tell him a thing or two for the way he's treated you."

"Don't worry about it," Anita said and started out of the room.

When she went downstairs Charles was waiting for her in the hallway. He said, "Mrs. Miller tells me you have a guest."

"Just Doris," she said. "You remember her. She's staying overnight."

He scowled. "That's very awkward," he said nervously. "I've just had word from the inspector that was the skeleton of the young man Amanda murdered. I'm planning to have a special seance tonight to try and reach her spirit again."

"Well?"

"We don't want a stranger here," he said angrily. "Doris wouldn't understand."

"I'm certain she will," she insisted. "In fact I'm sure she'll take part in the seance if we ask her." And as she said this a definite plan was forming in her mind. A plan she felt might help solve the mystery of the apparition.

CHAPTER TEN

Anita had been apprehensive of the reception her friend might receive at Shorecliff. All in all it worked out better than she'd hoped. Charles swiftly assumed all his old charm and was extremely nice to Doris, and Pat had executed another of her about-faces and received the visitor with what appeared to be sincere friendliness. Pat invited Doris to join the seance after dinner. Mary Vane had not come down for the evening meal and the word was that she had a headache and was resting for the seance.

Pat approached Doris when she was standing in the hallway with Anita and said, "Maybe you've heard we're having a seance tonight?"

"I think it was mentioned," Doris said politely.

"Charles would like you to join us in the circle," Pat went on. "That is if you have no serious objections to spiritualism."

Doris smiled. "I'm not a convert."

"Neither am I," Pat said frankly and glanced at Anita. "And I doubt whether Anita is. But we have been trying to contact the ghost of Amanda because Charles is planning this book about her."

"I don't mind joining in," Doris said. "I'm positive I won't be any help."

"You never can tell. The spirits behave in a strange fashion," Pat said. "I think Anita will bear me out in that."

"Very strange," Anita agreed. "Since coming to Shorecliff I've almost been convinced that we can contact those still earthbound. And Amanda seems to be among the group."

"Mary Vane does very well," Pat said. "I just hope she gets over her headache before it's time for the seance. Charles wants to try and contact Amanda while the news of the age of the skeleton is still fresh. We know now that it is that of the murdered captain. Charles hopes to get other information from her before he begins his book."

Doris knew how Pat had pushed to be Charles' assistant on the project but she gave no hint of this. She merely said, "Then you're working with Anita's husband on the project?"

Pat blushed slightly. "Yes. He asked me

to. I had so little to do at the time I hated to refuse."

"I'm sure you must be enjoying it," Doris said dryly.

"We've been working very hard," Pat said with a smile for Anita. "I'm certain Anita must often wonder what we're up to. We spend hours in the library digging into old books and letters and making notes."

Anita carried on the pretense. "I know how much it means to Charles," she said. "And since you've lived here all your life and know the house so well I'm sure you're best equipped to help him."

"That's very generous of you," Pat told her.

Doris frowned. "Don't you find this seance business a little spooky? I mean it's a strange old house anyway. Or should I say houses since there *are* two of them?"

"They've always gone by the joint name of Shorecliff," Anita said.

"When did you first learn of Amanda's ghost?" Doris asked.

"I was twelve," Pat said quietly. "Aunt Clare had just adopted me. I remember one winter evening she had guests and I was brought down to be shown off. There was a blazing log fire in the living room. Aunt Clare sat in front of it and told the story of Amanda. I was especially curious about the enamel face Amanda had brought back from Europe. I used to have nightmares and imagine I saw that face coming at me in the darkness."

"And now you believe you've actually been able to talk to her?" Doris said.

"Mary Vane brought us her message. The voice was unlike any I'd ever heard before and the location she gave us for finding the body turned out to be true."

"So now you want to try again?" Doris suggested.

"Charles has several questions he'd like answered," Pat said. "He hopes we may be fortunate enough to contact her at least one more time. I'll tell him you've agreed to cooperate," she said with a parting smile and went on her way to join Anita's husband in the library.

Anita gave her friend a knowing glance. "Shall we take a walk outside? It's such a nice evening."

"I'd love to," Doris agreed at once.

Outside they were free to talk without worrying about being overheard. As they strolled down the gravel path toward the cliff's edge, Anita asked, "Well, what do you make of Pat?"

Her friend gave her a wise glance. "She's

after Charles all right. And I doubt if she's the innocent little creature she likes to pretend. Pat could very well be the phantom Amanda who's harassing you."

"I know that," Anita admitted. "But I've never been able to establish any proof."

"You may eventually."

Anita frowned. "There's Mary Vane to be considered. You'll realize how clever she is when you meet her. And if I want to include all the suspicious types there's also Mrs. Miller and Aunt Clem."

"Mrs. Miller?" Doris questioned as they approached the end of the path and stood on the grassy surface of the cliff's edge. The setting sun was reflected on the sparkling blue of the ocean. A white-sailed pleasure craft moved lazily along far out on the water.

"The housekeeper," Anita said. "You must have noticed how grumpy she is. According to Pat she is the illegitimate sister of Aunt Clem and our late Aunt Clare. And she's always held a grudge because she was not recognized nor left anything in the will."

"But she's employed in the house," Doris said in wonderment. "Isn't that a little difficult?"

"I don't like the situation," she admitted.

"But she's been here for so long. I couldn't think of doing anything about it now."

Doris gave her a sympathetic look. "Meanwhile she moves around Shorecliff like a brooding Lady Macbeth. I don't envy you, Anita. What about your Aunt Clem?"

Anita smiled forlornly. "I'd say she was harmless enough. Also, she lives in the other house. She's elderly, very particular about the family name and honor and gives her son, Gordon, a rough time."

"In other words the estate is loaded with pleasant people!"

"If only this Amanda business was cleared up it might be all right here," she said. "As it stands now I'm living in terror."

Doris sighed. "I'm sorry I ever came. And I'm even sorrier I decided to stay overnight. When I leave I'm going to do nothing but worry about you."

"Don't feel that way," Anita said. "You've helped me just by being here. I'll manage somehow."

"What about this seance?" Doris asked. "Do you think they actually expect to reach that hundred-year-dead murderess?"

"It was a startling experience before. Mary Vane spoke in a voice quite unlike that of her guide, a child named Elsie. It was the kind of voice I'd imagine Amanda to have. And the things she said were what her ghost might have been expected to say."

Doris smiled sourly. "Did she give voice to her intention of taking over your husband?"

"Not openly. But it was there. Veiled in what she said," Anita worried. "Don't you think Charles looks bad? He's not his old self at all."

"He put on quite a show for me," Doris reminded her. "But I would say something is bothering him. I mean in addition to the attractive Pat."

Anita glanced back at the sprawling old mansion. "If there is any trickery going on I have the feeling we'll get an example of it tonight. I'm almost afraid to sit there in the darkness again."

"All the lights are out when the medium is at work?"

"Yes."

"That gives lots of opportunity for any kind of trickery," Doris said.

She nodded. "I know. I've had an idea in mind since Charles suggested you join the circle."

"Oh?"

"It's natural that you should sit next to me," Anita said. "While the seance is going on I'd like to slip away from the table. Then if anything happens I may be able to spot who is guilty. I'd like you to take my place."

Doris lifted her eyebrows. "How can I?"

"You could move into my chair and if there is any call to clasp hands with those on either side of you, you can lean over enough to bridge the gap of the empty chair. So no one will guess I've left."

"I don't know whether I like the idea," her friend said.

"It's my one chance to observe the seance objectively," Anita told her. "I'm sure it would be helpful."

Doris shrugged. "I'll try it if you like. Only don't blame me if anything goes wrong. I don't know a thing about seances."

"It will be all right," she assured her. "If you'll just do as I say." Looking back toward Shorecliff she saw that Gordon Morehouse was heading across the lawn to join them. "Here comes Gordon now."

The young man with the glasses had a smile as he came up to them. He wore a pair of gray trousers and blue sports blazer and looked very nice. "Good evening, ladies," he said. "I assume you've been asked to join in the happening tonight. Mary Vane is going to approach the spirits again."

"The invitations were out long ago," Anita said with a wry smile. "This is my friend, Doris Benson."

Gordon greeted her visitor warmly. "How wonderful for Anita that you should arrive at this time. Are you going to stay awhile?"

"Just overnight," Doris said.

Gordon turned to Anita. "Can't you persuade her to stay longer?"

"She's on vacation," Anita explained. "And she's joining a party in Maine tomorrow."

Gordon gave Doris a worried look. "That's too bad," he said. "Anita has probably told you about her illness."

"She has," Doris said.

"I think it would do her good to have an old friend around for a time," he went on.

"I can't understand these spells," Doris said. "Anita was never ill. The idea of her having convulsive fits comes as a shock to me."

"She's been going through an ordeal," Gordon said with meaning. "And she needs friends badly."

Anita was embarrassed by the turn the conversation had taken. In an attempt to change the subject she asked him, "Is your mother going to join the circle tonight?"

He shook his head. "Mother has been in a state ever since the last seance. She refuses point blank to have anything more to do with Mary Vane."

"Perhaps she's wise," Anita mused.

"I hope she'll leave after this business tonight," Gordon said. "Perhaps then Mother will be in a better humor."

If Mary Vane had any intention of leaving there was nothing of it in her manner when she entered the living room an hour later to lead the seance. She was wearing her usual black dress and pearls and Anita realized this drab garb would make it easier for her to move about in the darkness to create her illusions.

With an air of authority Mary Vane marched over to the table and in her hollow voice, said, "Now if you will all take your places, please."

Charles, looking as haggard as before, saw to it that everyone had a chair. He helped seat Doris next to Anita without seemingly taking any notice of the arrangement. Anita gave her friend a knowing look to advise her she intended to follow through with her plan.

Mary Vane's gaunt, attractive face was pale and the dark hollows under her eyes even more pronounced. She studied them all and then said, "Tonight may be the most important of all our attempts at materialization. We may not manage to see the spirit of Amanda Shore. But I hope we may at least hear her voice again."

Charles nodded and addressed them all, "We know now the murder was committed. But I'd like to learn more of the reasons for the crime. And how Amanda felt about it in her declining years when she knew many people believed her to be a murderess."

Anita looked across the room at the portrait of the dead woman and once again experienced an eerie feeling. Those strange eyes still held a weird power. She felt very tense. In a few minutes the lights would be turned out and she would have to watch for her chance to slip from the circle and take a stand by the doorway. She felt this would give her an excellent opportunity to check any movements in the room.

"Please turn the lights out," Mary Vane said in her sepulchral voice.

Charles rose to switch the lights off this

time. And then Anita heard him coming back in the darkness to take his seat. She realized she would have to move much more softly if her plan was to be successful.

"Join hands, please," Mary Vane said.

Patricia was on one side of Anita and Doris on the other. She took each of their hands as a distinct silence came over the room. While they were still holding hands the medium said, "We would speak with Amanda Shore! Amanda, if you hear me, give us some evidence of your being here." There was another protracted silence.

And then loudly in the darkness came a single rap on the table. It was followed after a few seconds by another rap and then a third. Mary Vane said, "So you are here, Amanda! Speak to us!"

Almost at once the medium began to moan. The moaning went on at intervals and as usual at this period in the seance they released hands and Anita was free to move out of the circle. She touched Doris on the arm lightly as a signal and then very quietly rose from her chair and backed away from the group.

It was fortunate that her movements were masked by the groans from the medium. And then suddenly the voice she had heard before, the voice identified as Amanda's called out clearly, "Why are you seeking me?"

Anita backed quickly to the doorway and stood there, trembling a little. The events of the circle seemed even weirder once she had disassociated herself from it.

Charles spoke up, "We found the captain's skeleton."

"I knew you would," Amanda said.

"Have you no regrets?" Charles asked.

"None," the ghostly voice answered. "I wanted you to find the body. And I have no shame for my deed. He deserved to die!"

"Didn't you ever feel sorry when you were old?" Charles asked the spirit.

"I was never old," the spirit voice said scornfully. "I found the secret of eternal youth!"

"You mean the mask?" he said.

There was a moment of silence and Anita had the strange feeling that someone had brushed by her. She couldn't be sure but she was almost certain. There had been some kind of movement in the blackness of the big room. She pressed close to the wall. Perhaps Mary Vane had perfected the art of ventriloquism and so could move about the room at will at the same time her voice appeared to be emanating from her regular place.

"How they stared at me!" Amanda gloated. "They had never seen beauty so preserved before. I was never to show another wrinkle."

"Were your last days happy?" Charles wanted to know.

Again there was a long silence. Anita stared into the shadowed dark of the living room, straining for some sign of movement. But beyond the odd feeling that someone was moving about she had no way of confirming her suspicions. And she began to think that perhaps it was the spirit presence of Amanda that had gone by her like a fleeting breeze. Perhaps the evil spirit that had so often attacked her was at large in the room.

"When I was old I wept tears of loneliness," the husky voice of Amanda went on. "They streamed down my lovely cheeks. But they did not mar my beauty! Because my beauty would last forever!"

"Are you content to move on to a higher level now?" Charles asked. "Must you still be earthbound?"

"One day in the mirror," the voice went on, ignoring his question and with a touch of horror in her tone now, "one day in the mirror I saw myself too clearly. My face had the beauty of a rare china piece but my eyes were old and sunken in their sockets! I was old and ugly!"

"But that is all over now," Charles said, his own voice sounding taut and weary.

"And that night I killed myself!" Amanda said brokenly. "I took a powder that I had saved carefully for another. And then it was over. They never guessed. Old age was the doctor's verdict. But it was loneliness and remorse that had taken its toll. You must tell them that! That I killed myself in atonement."

"I will put it down in the book," Charles promised. "But there is no proof?"

"You have my word," Amanda said. "I have crossed the bridge of another world to tell you. Because you are my devoted! You have been picked to pass on my message. You will tell them the truth at last!"

"I will do all that," Charles promised. "I regard it a sacred duty. What other secrets do you have to reveal to me?"

There was silence again. And Anita held her breath as she sensed a figure moving across in front of her. And then there was a scream! A female scream! Bloodcurdling in its terror!

Pandemonium broke loose in the circle.

There were quick, angry cries, male and female voices mingling and as Anita stood there frozen with fear Charles switched the lights on. He saw her standing there and registered amazement. But all this was lost in the discovery of Doris Benson slumped on the floor. Anita screamed and ran across to the stricken girl.

Gordon Morehouse was already by her and raising her in his arms. Doris opened her eyes and stared at the people gathered around her. Her plain face was pale and she looked thoroughly shaken.

"My throat!" she gasped. "Cold hands on my throat!"

Anita felt a surge of guilt. Doris had seated herself in her chair at her bidding. And those icy hands had been meant to grasp her throat. She gave thanks that her friend had suffered no worse injury.

Gordon asked the stricken girl, "Are you telling us someone tried to choke you?"

"Yes," Doris said.

"But that's impossible," Pat said. "No one could get in here to do that."

Mary Vane was on her feet, looking enraged that her seance had been interrupted. "It shouldn't be hard to pin the blame on the proper person," she said. And to Anita, "Why did you leave the circle? What were you doing by the door-way?"

"I jumped up and stepped back when she screamed," Anita said, knowing they very likely wouldn't believe her.

But no one seemed ready to argue the point. Instead they gave their attention to Doris who was now being helped to her feet. The dark girl flashed a warning glance to say nothing.

Charles came up to her saying, "It's too bad your friend was so hysterical. She ruined the seance."

"I disagree," she told him. "I think you managed very well before she screamed."

"We could have done much more," Charles said, his burning eyes showing anger.

Mary Vane came to join them. "There is no use trying again tonight," she said. "The mood has been completely destroyed." And she turned her back on them and marched out of the room.

It struck Anita that the medium had been suspiciously anxious to leave. Was she determined to go before any further embarrassing questions were asked? If someone had moved around to try and choke Doris it had to be a member of the circle — either that or the icy fingers of an actual ghost had taken her in their grasp.

Anita went over to her friend. "I'll take you up to your room," she said, placing an arm around her.

Doris gave her a grateful look. "I do feel awful."

Charles had also come forward and now he questioned the girl, "What about the hands you claim tried to choke you? Surely you were wrong! You undoubtedly had a fit of hysterics."

"I have never been to a seance before. It was a strain," the girl said in an apologetic manner.

"It is too bad you didn't think of that before you agreed to attend," Charles said angrily. "Our seance was cut off in the middle."

"I disagree," Anita said quickly. "Anyway it isn't important now. Please excuse us." And she led Doris to the doorway.

As soon as they reached Doris' bedroom and shut the door, the girl turned to Anita with a frightened look. "Hands did grip my throat! Clammy cold hands! I wasn't hysterical! I didn't imagine it!"

"I know you didn't," Anita agreed quietly. "And those hands were meant for my throat. Remember you'd moved into my chair."

"So I had," Doris said as the thought had its full impact on her. "The ghost was trying to settle with you!"

"If it was a ghost."

"That seance shocked me," Doris admitted. "I honestly think that Vane woman can communicate with the dead."

"Or else she's clever enough to give a thorough impression she can," Anita said grimly. "I was convinced something passed me in the darkness just before you screamed."

Doris stared at her wide-eyed. "Amanda's ghost?"

"I wonder," she said softly.

"So you didn't really discover anything."

"No. And I put you in real danger," Anita said unhappily. "I'm so sorry."

"It doesn't matter." Doris sat on her bed in the soft light of the room's single dresser lamp and her face showed the strain of the experience she'd just gone through. She shivered. "That ghost voice! It made my flesh creep!"

"I know."

Doris frowned. "This is a dreadful place, Anita. I can well imagine why you think Charles is under some kind of spell. You should get away from here."

"How can I?"

"Just go!"

"Not until I know more about what is happening."

"Then it may be too late!" her friend protested. "You heard what that voice said tonight. There was murder and then suicide. Amanda killed herself!"

"The newest link added to the chain," Anita said bitterly. "I hope Charles is satisfied at last."

"He seemed very angry that I screamed."

"That's typical of his mood these days," Anita warned her.

"Perhaps there is a ghost," Doris said. "And if so, what can you hope to do? You'll never be able to protect yourself. Why not leave with me in the morning?"

"I can't go and leave Charles."

"Why not? If he has no more consideration than to keep you here in this place he ought to be left alone!"

Anita nodded. "I realize you're right. But I'll have to work this out my own way."

She stayed with her friend until it was almost midnight. When she went downstairs there wasn't a sign of anyone. All the lights in the living room had been turned off but the hallway light still burned brightly. She advanced to the doorway of the living room and stared into its semidarkness.

A faint glimmer of light from the hallway touched Amanda's portrait so the arrogant face stared back at her through the shadows in a curious manner. Anita stood there with her eyes fixed on the lovely, cold face of the beauty who had murdered to satisfy her vanity and who'd only found a release from her unhappiness in suicide.

How long after the portrait had been painted did she journey to France for that curious treatment? When had her chill beauty so deteriorated that she could no longer face the ravage of wrinkles and faded skin? And how much confidence was restored to her when that enamel mask was finally applied to her aging face? She had come back to Shorecliff with that odd, expressionless beauty which had created so much comment.

Yet in the end the artificial mask could not save her. The sunken eyes and shrunken body, along with thinning gray hair, must have made the artificial face seem like the grotesque thing it was. And when she knew that all was lost she saw how far her vanity had led her. She had murdered the only man she loved and tried to stave off age with a porcelain face. Both times she had been terribly wrong and because she could not live with the knowledge she ended her life.

A board creaked behind Anita and she wheeled around suddenly. Mrs. Miller stood behind her with a sardonic smile.

She said, "They have all gone. I hear the seance was not a success."

"Not completely," she said, trying to hide the fact she'd been frightened from the housekeeper.

"They'll have no luck with that one," Mrs. Miller prophesied.

"What one?"

Mrs. Miller jerked her head toward Amanda's portrait. "Her! She hates them all!"

"Do you really think that?" Anita couldn't help being curious at the strange reaction of the illegitimate member of the Shore family.

"She was an outcast after that captain vanished," the old woman said. "I heard about it from someone who knew."

"Really."

The sour face showed satisfaction. "I could tell you more about this house and its people than most."

"You have been here a long while."

"All my life," Mrs. Miller said simply. "I

worked on the estate farm until my man died. Then I came to Shorecliff."

"You must be very devoted to the family," Anita said, wanting to see what the old woman would say, wondering whether she might suddenly blurt out that she was also of the family.

Mrs. Miller's eyes became as cold as those in Amanda's portrait. She was startled by the sudden likeness between them. And in her bitter way the housekeeper said, "I don't consider what is left today real family. You'll pardon my saying that since I know you and your husband now own Shorecliff. But he was only here a little time when he was a lad."

"I realize that," she said.

"The rest of them don't count, either," Mrs. Miller went on. "Miss Patricia is only adopted. She'll leave here one day and never come back, especially now that you've got the house. And as for the others in the house next door they're not going to be here much longer either."

"Why do you say that?"

The sour face took on a sneer. "Clem is close to the dying age and just holding on. That Gordon is a weakling who has drained his mother of nearly all her money. And she's been willing to let him ruin her as long as she's managed to keep him under her thumb!"

Anita smiled grimly. "You don't think much of any of us, do you?"

"It's no one's fault," the old woman asserted. "There's a curse on this old house and on the Shore family. Some say it began with Amanda. But I know there were other sinners down through the years. And now the time has come for the reckoning." The old woman nodded goodnight and went on down the shadowed dark hall.

Anita watched after her, a fresh sensation of fear coloring her thoughts. Mrs. Miller had talked as if they were all doomed. Almost as if she personified the avenging angel. Could she have become so mad in her bitterness as to have taken on the role of the phantom Amanda?

CHAPTER ELEVEN

Doris Benson left early the following morning. It was only the fact she had promised to meet her friends that made her go. She gave Anita her address in Maine and urged her to call her if the situation at Shorecliff should get any worse. Anita told her friend not to worry and put on the best possible front although she hated to see her leave. So she was left alone to deal with the others in the forbidding old mansion.

The morning was wet and foggy and suited her somber mood. Pat and Charles were working in the library again and she settled down in the living room with a magazine. She'd only been reading a few minutes when the phone rang. It was Aunt Clem.

"I wish you'd come over," the old woman said in her nervous, high-pitched fashion. "I want someone to talk to."

Anita felt rather sorry for Aunt Clem so she said, "All right. I'll come for awhile now."

"That's good of you, dear," Aunt Clem said. "And please don't say anything to the others. I don't want to talk to any of them."

She was curious as to why Aunt Clem should suddenly want to talk to anyone. She'd been quite content to shut herself off from the entire household since the night Amanda had first spoken at the seance. Slipping on her raincoat and kerchief she went out and hurried across the lawn to the other entrance. Aunt Clem was there waiting to let her in. She thought the old woman looked even more pinched and white than usual. And the blue shawl she wore over her shoulders made her appear much more elderly.

She fussed over Anita, taking her coat to hang up on the rack in the hallway. The Morehouse section of Shorecliff was not as elaborately furnished as the other house but the ornate woodwork and plaster ceilings were identical.

Aunt Clem led her to a small sitting room at the rear of the house. A coffee percolator was already set out on a table along with cups and a tray with cookies. The old woman seated herself and sighed. "This is my retreat. It's the one truly cozy room in this whole house."

Anita glanced around the modestly furnished room, taking in the gray and white floral drapes at the tall single window. The window looked out on the yard and stable buildings. Just now it was streaked with rivulets of rain.

"It's a nice room," she said.

Aunt Clem nodded. She poured a cup of coffee and passed it to her. "Just help yourself to cream, sugar and the cookies," she said.

"I'm glad you called me," Anita said. "My friend left this morning and I'm feeling depressed."

"I can well understand it," the old woman said, her face a picture of despair over her coffee cup. "Of course you know what went on last night. More scandal has been added. Now that woman claims Amanda Shore was a suicide."

"I know," she said, sipping her coffee.

Aunt Clem shook her head. "Why did I bring her here in the first place?"

"Weren't you trying to get in touch with Aunt Clare's spirit?"

"I was," the old woman admitted with a sigh. "It was my opinion Clare hadn't been considerate of Gordon and me in her will. But we never did reach her to ask her any questions. I think that Mary Vane deliber-

252

ately made it as difficult as possible."

"She is a strange person," Anita admitted.

"There is a great deal of evil about her." Aunt Clem frowned. "She asked for an exorbitant amount to come down here in the first place. And now I'm sure she must be costing your husband a great deal of money."

"I don't know what arrangement Charles has with her."

"Gordon claims she exerts a strong influence over him. And I warn you as long as there's money coming her way she'll go on getting messages from beyond. I believe the woman is a charlatan."

"You couldn't have thought that before or you wouldn't have brought her down here."

"I didn't," the old woman admitted. "But I know better now."

Anita said, "I've talked to Charles about her. But he's very unreasonable these days."

Aunt Clem gave a deep sigh. "I'm sorry for you, my dear. Have you had any more of those dreadful spells?"

"No. I'm sure they were brought on some way," she said. "Perhaps sheer terror caused them. Each time I had an attack it was after seeing the ghost."

The old woman's pale blue eyes searched her face. "You did see Amanda's ghost then?"

"Several times. I'll never forget that weird china mask. It was horrible!"

Aunt Clem looked troubled. "I believe I have seen her myself. But of course Shorecliff is peopled with ghosts and phantoms. It is a house of shadows."

"I'd like to leave it," she said. "But Charles won't go now. He's obsessed with doing this book on Amanda."

"That evil woman!" Aunt Clem put her empty cup on the table. "We'll all be disgraced when these stories are printed in the press. And they most certainly will be."

"But she lived so long ago. Surely her actions won't have much interest now."

"Don't you believe it," the old woman cautioned. "People like scandal, no matter what the vintage."

"I suppose so."

"I don't understand how this Mary Vane gets all her information. It's been whispered for years that Amanda was a suicide but nothing was openly said. Now this so-called medium tells the story for everyone to hear."

"I wouldn't worry too much," Anita advised.

"One can't help but worry when the honor of the family is at stake," Aunt Clem said with particular obstinacy. "I do wish you'd try and exert some influence on Charles and force him to send her packing back to Boston."

"I've tried with no luck."

Aunt Clem frowned. "That Pat is one to watch. You must know that. The girl has no morals at all."

"I didn't realize that." Anita was surprised at the venom of the old woman's attack on Clare's adopted daughter.

"She hates me and I don't care!" the old woman said.

"Why should she hate you?"

"Because of Gordon. She wanted to snare him. But I soon put a stop to that. Of course she's never forgiven me. But imagine my Gordon throwing himself away on an ordinary little creature like her!"

"She is attractive," Anita ventured, knowing she was in danger of arousing the old woman's anger with any favorable comment about the brown-haired girl.

"Beauty is only skin deep!" the old woman said with disgust. "I suppose now that she knows she can't get Gordon she's after your husband."

"I doubt if there's anything serious between Charles and her."

"Don't be too sure," Aunt Clem warned. "You never can tell with men. They do the most awful things. I've had my problems with Gordon, trying to make a gentleman of him and stop him from messing up his life."

Anita thought she should put her thoughts to the old woman frankly. So she asked, "Don't you want Gordon to marry?"

"Of course I do," the old woman said crossly. "But I would like to see him established first and choose between a few girls of his own social class, not a Patricia Shore!"

"I see," she said quietly. She knew that Gordon's mother had no intention of allowing him to marry anyone. There would be no new mistress of the house while she lived.

"So you must really take care," the old woman warned. "If she thinks Charles might divorce you she'll plague him until he does. That's the sort she is!"

"But Aunt Clare left her plenty even though she hasn't the house."

"The little snip thought she'd get it all,"

Aunt Clem said scornfully. "She was badly upset when she heard you and Charles were coming to take possession."

"I'm sorry it wasn't left to her," she sighed.

"Or to those who were more entitled to it."

"Mrs. Miller claims the family is doomed and the house is cursed," Anita said with a forlorn smile. "I'm beginning to agree with her."

"She's another one to be careful of. Hateful old woman!"

"But she has been here a long while as housekeeper."

"Entirely too long," Aunt Clem said angrily. "My father should never have installed her here. It wasn't fair to Clare or me. But he didn't care. He was a wicked, willful man!"

Anita was tempted to tell her she knew the truth about Mrs. Miller but thought the better of it. With Aunt Clem in such an angry state about impending scandal it would hardly be diplomatic to remind her she had an illegitimate sister living in the house.

She got up. "I'd better go now," she said. "Thanks for the coffee. It helped on this unpleasant morning."

Aunt Clem was on her feet as well. She glanced toward the window. "I'd say it was going to be an all day rain."

"I'm sure you're right," she said. "I hope Charles doesn't get any more ideas about holding seances tonight. I couldn't stand another so soon — especially in this depressing weather."

"I fully agree. Mary Vane should go," Aunt Clem declared as they went to the front door. "And do keep me informed as to what is going on. Gordon tells me so little and I have a right to know."

Anita said goodbye to the pathetic old woman and went back to her own section of the house. As it was getting near noon she decided to go straight up to the bedroom and prepare for lunch. She met no one on the way up but when she reached the door of the room she had a sudden feeling of uneasiness.

Something warned her that the unexpected might happen, that she was not alone in the quiet corridor of the old mansion. Hesitantly touching her hand to the door knob she turned it and went inside. And standing by her dresser looking startled was the medium, Mary Vane.

Mary Vane spoke first, "I was looking for you," she said in her assured way. She was wearing the same black dress of the night before but there were no pearls at her neck.

"Were you?" she said coldly, angry at the intrusion.

"I suppose you think I shouldn't be in here," the medium said, boldly facing up to her.

"It is the bedroom of my husband and myself," she said. "And I am surprised to find you here."

Mary Vane smiled coldly. "You needn't be. I have your husband's permission."

"You what?"

"Your husband told me I could come here," the medium said. "You can check with him if you like. He'll tell you the same thing."

Anita's indignation was growing. "Why should he tell you such a thing?"

"I'm engaged in psychical research," she said. "You have spoken of seeing Amanda's ghost in this room."

"What has that got to do with it?"

"I'm sensitive to such things," the gauntly attractive woman said suavely. "I came in here during your absence to see if I could sense the presence of an apparition."

"I'll ask you not to come again."

Mary Vane shrugged. "Just as you say. I'll have to report you to your husband as not being willing to help."

"I don't care what you report!" Anita declared. "Please leave this room."

Mary Vane walked slowly to the door and turned for a final word, "You're being very foolish. I hope you realize that."

Anita didn't dare to make any reply. She was too enraged. She stood in silence as the medium went out and closed the door after her. Then reaction set in and she threw herself on the bed and sobbed. How could Charles be so thoughtless of her as to tactlessly send this strange woman to her room when she was out of the house!

After she'd wiped away her tears she began to think of how she'd go about protecting herself. And she remembered the gun! The gun Gordon had been kind enough to provide her with. She'd been afraid to use it and had hidden it away and forgotten about it. Now she began to consider the weapon with new feelings. She might be very wise to keep it under her pillow at night, ready to use.

She suddenly realized that the gun might have been spirited away by her enemies. To check she dragged a chair over to the closet and searched the hat box where she'd hidden the gun. Slipping the top off the round box she fumbled inside. In a second her hand touched its cold metal. It was safe where she'd put it. She decided to let it remain there until just before she went to bed. Then she'd take it out and hide it under the pillow before Charles came up to join her. He never came to bed until long after she did. And often he would get up in the middle of the night and roam restlessly about like a sleepwalker.

It was all a part of his alarming mental picture. She was convinced he was ill as well as being obsessed with legend of Amanda. And she saw little hope of his improving unless they somehow got away from the sinister atmosphere of the old mansion. In the meantime she would at least have the gun to give herself a small amount of added protection.

The day continued wet and seemed to drag endlessly. She missed chatting with Doris. In the short space of her stay they had spent a great deal of time together. The others in the old house, including Charles, seemed to be behaving deliberately coldly to her. She waited until after lunch when Charles was alone in the library.

Then she went in and closed the door after her before she stood facing him across the cluttered desk.

"What are you trying to do?" she demanded. "Make me have a nervous breakdown?"

He scowled up at her. "Must you annoy me about such nonsense?"

His face looked haggard and sick but his words drowned all the pity his appearance had produced. Staring at him coldly, she said, "When I returned to my room this morning Mary Vane was in it."

"I know," he said.

"She claimed you told her she could go in there."

"I did. It was for research purposes. I didn't think you'd object!"

"Then you're wrong!" she said sharply. "I object to that and all the other weird things you're dabbling in here. Those seances have got to end."

He seemed astonished. "Why do you say that?"

"They're disrupting the peace here and accomplishing nothing. I have some say as your wife. And I tell you Mary Vane has to go."

He regarded her in silence for a moment. "Who put you up to this? Aunt Clem? I understand you were over there this morning."

"You keep close tabs on me, don't you?"

"I find it pays," her husband said. "Now will you please end this bickering and leave me to my work."

"I'll go when I please," she said. "I never see you anymore. Pat is always with you. And you never come up to the bedroom until I'm asleep. We might as well be strangers living apart."

"If I annoy you coming up late at night I'll have Mrs. Miller fix me another room," he said stiffly. "I've been thinking about it anyhow."

It wasn't what she had wanted at all. "I didn't say you annoyed me," she protested. "But I would like a chance to talk with you occasionally."

"So you could battle with me as you're doing now," he said disgustedly. "Why are you so anxious to stop me from doing my book?"

"Because I think Amanda is not a proper subject for you. Let someone else outside the family write it."

"You'd like that," he said coldly. "You'd like me to miss this really marvelous opportunity."

"Is it marvelous if it means breaking us

up?" she said in quieter tone.

"Aren't you the one who is bringing us dangerously close to that?"

"I think not!" she said.

Charles looked at her with troubled eyes. "I wouldn't have been able to have forgiven you as much as I have if I hadn't known you were ill. You've never been the same since those attacks."

"I believe someone here gave me some kind of drug!"

"That's hardly likely," he said.

"I've never been sick like that before."

"Which doesn't prove anything but that you're sick now. Please go, Anita, I'm way behind in this work." His voice had taken on a pleading note.

"All right," she said bitterly. "I know you much prefer Pat."

She went out, leaving him staring after her with unhappy eyes. Hurrying down the corridor she almost bumped into Pat who was apparently on her way to join Charles in the library. Pat smiled smugly and continued on her way. Anita felt the situation couldn't get much worse.

The rain ended at six o'clock but the fog hung on. By eight o'clock it was almost dark. And the heavy, dripping fog cloaked everything. The old mansion seemed more like a haunted castle than ever.

She spent nearly all the evening in the living room with a novel. She thought she might hear from Gordon but the hours passed and there was no word. He often didn't come home until late. He would attend auctions in Portsmouth and go out on scouting trips for additional items for his antique shop.

When ten-thirty came her eyes were drooping with sleep. She marked the book where she'd left off, put it aside, then went upstairs to her room. When she got there she was surprised to see that Charles' brush and comb were gone from the dresser top. A swift examination of the drawers showed that his shirts had been removed. She hurried to the closet and saw that all his clothes were gone. So he'd made good his threat and moved to another room.

It was a nasty blow. She'd felt at least some comfort in knowing he was there with her for most of the night. Now she was going to be completely alone. He'd used this small excuse to abandon her in this cruel fashion. She was beginning to doubt if he had the slightest love for her any longer. He treated her like an enemy.

Now there was no question of her

arming herself for the night. She changed for bed and took the gun down from its hiding place and unlocked the safety catch. Then she very cautiously placed it under her pillow. It would be available in a moment and while she'd had no experience in using it she had an idea just firing a shot would be helpful whether it hit its target or not. It would at least arouse the others in the house.

In spite of her earlier weariness she now had trouble falling asleep. Her thoughts were tormented by the cruelty Charles was showing towards her. She felt she could never feel the same about him when this was over, if the danger ever should end. Right now it seemed it might go on forever. At last she fell into a restless sleep.

The heavy perfume of Attar of Roses seemed to be drowning her. It filled her nostrils and her lungs.

She screamed and sat up.

At first she was so confused by being roused from her sleep that she hardly realized what was happening. The strong odor of rose perfume swirled about her and warned her of an intruder. In the darkness she saw a shape forming in the far corner near the fireplace. Gradually the shining porcelain face of Amanda became clear. And the phantom creature that had attacked her before was slowly making its way towards her bed.

Her heart was beating wildly and she was still paralyzed by fear. But as the stench of the rose perfume grew stronger and the apparition came closer she broke the spell and fumbled under her pillow for the gun. Her trembling hand almost dropped it and she had a fresh fear the gun might accidentally go off and wound her. But she finally got it properly in her hand and pointed it at the expressionless face of Amanda as it swayed toward her through the darkness.

Her eyes automatically closed as she fired. The bullet blazed out but she could not tell whether or not she'd hit her target. There was no sign of the phantom . . . only the strong perfume of Attar of Roses remained as proof the ghost had been there.

But the sound of the shot had served exactly as she'd anticipated. A clamor of voices came from the corridor and a moment later there was pounding on her door. She threw on her dressing gown and opened the door.

Charles entered in robe and pajamas. "I heard a shot," he said.

"Yes," she nodded. "It came from in here."

He looked startled. "You have a gun?"

"Yes."

"Where did you get it?"

"A friend got it for me," she said, deciding that it would be best not to implicate Gordon.

"Give it to me," Charles ordered, his hand stretched out to take it.

She took a step back and shook her head. "No!"

He stared at her in a strange way. "Do I have to take it from you?"

"Try that and I'll use it again," she warned him, the gun raised in her hand.

Charles seemed nonplussed. "I believe you really mean it!"

"I do! I promise you!" she said.

He hesitated a moment, uncertain of what to do or say next. Then swallowing hard, he asked, "What were you shooting at just now?"

"Amanda."

"Amanda!" He echoed the name in a startled tone.

"Yes. Her ghost or whatever it is that has been attacking me appeared in the corner over there," she pointed toward the fireplace. "I was too frightened to do anything

268

at first. But when I saw that awful enamel face coming closer to me I got out the gun and fired."

Charles gave her a significant look. "You had it under your pillow?"

"I needed something after you left me here alone."

"I see," he said sarcastically. Then he walked over in the direction of the fireplace. He carefully examined the area where the ghost had first appeared for a moment and pointed to a spot fairly high on the paneled wall. "There's where your bullet is lodged."

"Anyway it scared away the phantom," she said. "It vanished at once."

Her husband's haggard face showed annoyance as he came back to her. "All right," he said. "You've had your fun. Now you'd better let me have that gun."

She maintained her stand. "No," she said. "As long as I remain in this house I intend to keep it."

He frowned. "You're in no fit mental state to be in possession of a gun. If I make a complaint to the police they'll come here and take it from you."

"Try that," she suggested. "I'll have a thing or two to tell them."

Charles regarded her with sullen eyes.

"All right," he said. "You can keep it for the night. But we'll have to settle this in the morning." And he left without another word.

She locked the door after him and leaned against it. She stared at the gun. Standing up to Charles had taken all her courage. But there had been no choice. She couldn't allow herself to go unprotected again. There was too much evil in the old mansion. At least the gun had saved her from the horror of another attack by the phantom figure tonight. It might do so again.

Before she went downstairs in the morning she hid the gun more carefully than before. She found a small open space in the bathroom floor which was concealed by the bathtub. And in this crevice she hid the gun. She pushed the gun to one side so that it could not be seen even by those who noticed the hole. Only a hand as small as her own could reach in to retrieve it again. She went downstairs satisfied that not even Mrs. Miller would find it.

Charles was waiting for her. He rose from his chair at the long table where he had been having breakfast with Pat. "Where's that gun?" he asked. "You promised to bring it down."

"I promised no such thing," she said.

"In any case I want it," her husband warned her.

She gave him a taunting smile. "I'm sorry. I haven't got it any longer."

He stared at her angrily. "All right," he said. "If that's the way you want it. I'll find it if it's anywhere up there."

"I'm sure you will," she said sweetly.

Pat, who had not said a word during all this, gave Charles a concerned look, and turning to Anita, said, "I think you would be wise to do as Charles says. He's only interested in your welfare."

"And I suppose that's what concerns you?" Anita said.

Pat blushed and avoided her eyes. Giving her attention to her plate, she said, "It's really none of my business, I suppose."

So the state of siege in which she lived with her husband and the others was to continue. Anita kept up a pretense of nonchalance even though she was as depressed as before. It was too humiliating to have Charles treat her this way in front of Pat. It was heartbreaking!

She'd no sooner left the breakfast table when Mrs. Miller came to tell her there was a long distance call for her. She took it

271

in the hallway and was startled to hear Doris Benson's voice on the other end of the line.

"I thought you were in Maine," she said.

"I was. But I came up here last night," her friend said. "I'm in Portsmouth. And I've been talking to someone who is interested in you."

"Who?" she said.

"Inspector Decker. I've told him my story and he seems to believe it. He wants you to come up and see him this morning. I'll wait here for you."

She hesitated. "I don't know whether I can get the car."

"More trouble with Charles?"

"I'm afraid so," she said.

"Get transportation some way," Doris said. "If you can't rent a taxi I'll come for you."

"Don't bother," Anita said. "I'll find a way." And she hung up.

The message had come as a distinct surprise to her. She'd never dreamed of Doris involving herself in the trouble again. She supposed that her friend was still worried after reaching Maine and decided to return and talk to Inspector Decker. It might mean a great deal, Anita realized, especially if Doris told the story of the attack on her at the seance and the inspector believed her. It might open the way for him to consider her version of events at Shorecliff to be true.

She knew that Charles would never give her permission to use the car in his angry mood and so she waited until he'd gone upstairs. And then she rushed out, got into the car and hurriedly started it. She drove quickly around the stables and headed for the main road. By the time she was safely away from the house she had come to a decision.

She would stop by Gordon's antique shop and tell him of her experiences of the night. And she would also ask his advice concerning what she'd say to the police.

CHAPTER TWELVE

As she drove to the antique shop Anita tried to sort things out in her mind. She knew she had angered Charles by refusing to surrender the gun but she was convinced she was right. The truth was her husband was a completely different person from the man she'd married. His macabre obsession with the long dead Amanda might be the explanation, and an evil influence from that other spirit world could have taken hold of him. If so, she knew of no way to combat it.

Or there might be a much more mundane and reasonable explanation of his strangeness. He might merely be suffering further after-effects of his serious accident of a year ago. He had not been completely well when he'd made the journey to Shorecliff and his condition could have worsened. Where Pat fitted into the picture was also hard to say. The brown-haired girl had been piqued at not being given Shorecliff and perhaps she was seeking revenge by posing as Amanda's phantom.

She stopped in front of the yard of the big white barn. Gordon must have seen her drive up for he came out before she could leave the car. He was smartly dressed in houndstooth slacks, a gray jacket and a black turtleneck sweater.

His sensitive, romantic face showed concern. "Something wrong?"

She nodded. "I used the gun you gave me last night. I thought I saw the ghost."

Gordon's brow furrowed. "Then Charles knows you have it?"

"I'm afraid so."

"Did he ask you for it?"

"Yes. But I refused to let him have it. I've hidden it securely."

"Smart girl!" Gordon said, looking less strained. "One of the reasons I gave it to you was to protect yourself in the event he attacked you."

She looked up at him with a new understanding in her eyes, a solemn realization of what had been happening. "You were the first one to make me aware of the danger," she admitted. "It was when you first talked to me about the gun that I knew Charles might harm me. That he'd had some sort of breakdown."

"He has to be ill," Gordon said grimly. "Or else Mary Vane has invoked the spirit of Amanda to take control of him."

"He's insane on the subject of Amanda."

"I know." The young antique dealer's eyes were troubled. "Either way he can be dangerous. Hold on to that gun and use it if you have to."

"I will," she promised. "Just now I'm on my way to Portsmouth to talk with Inspector Decker. My friend, Doris Benson, called me. She is waiting for me at the inspector's office." She hesitated. "I'm worried about what to say."

"Stick to the truth!" Gordon warned her. "Inspector Decker is clever. If you try lying to him he'll catch on fast."

"I wish I knew what the truth was!"

"You must have some strong opinions."

She caressed the rim of the car wheel a silent moment and pursed her lips. "I'd have to say I'm beginning to believe in that other world. That haven of the dead from which Mary Vane's voices come."

"Then tell him that," Gordon advised.

She smiled crookedly. "And he'll be agreeing with Dr. Wilson I'm the one with a twisted mind."

"You'll have to chance that."

"I've lost hope the inspector can do anything," she said. "But I owe it to Doris to go see him."

"She has gone to some pains to help you," he agreed.

"Thanks," she said with a faint smile. "I wanted to let you know."

He reached into the car and took her hand in his. The handsome face showed strain. "Anita, what about us?" he asked urgently.

"I don't know," she sighed.

"How can you love Charles after what's been going on?"

"I'm confused. If he's truly ill or under some horrible spell I oughtn't to blame him."

"But you should free yourself of him," Gordon insisted, his grip on her hand becoming almost cruelly firm. "I'm in love with you. I want to marry you."

"Please, Gordon! Later!"

"You're in great danger at Shorecliff," he warned. "Don't make your decision too late."

She looked up at him. "I appreciate all you've done."

Gordon smiled sadly. "I often wonder why I'm always cast in the loser's role."

"But you needn't be!" she protested. "I'm sure Pat would have married you if your mother hadn't caused trouble."

"Mother hasn't actually sweetened my life," he admitted. "That's another story."

"They'll be waiting. I must go."

He stepped back from the car. "Best of luck!"

He stood watching after her as she drove away. His look of utter sadness depressed her. She knew how much he had tried to help her. And he had made no secret of his love for her.

In fifteen minutes she reached State Police Headquarters at Portsmouth. Inside she was ushered into the same small office where she'd first met with Inspector Decker. He was standing by his desk; Doris Benson was seated.

"We were worried about you," Doris said.

The inspector waved her to the remaining empty chair. "Please sit down, Mrs. Shore." He glanced at Doris and then at her again before saying, "Your friend has offered me some interesting information."

"Oh?" Anita said warily.

"That must have been a startling seance you had at Shorecliff the other night."

"They've all been frightening," she admitted.

The tall man with the graying temples

frowned. "According to Miss Benson someone tried to choke her in the darkness. She'd taken your place in the circle. So they must have thought they were strangling you."

"Perhaps so," was her cautious reply.

"This more or less gives credence to the rather wild stories of attacks you mentioned before," he said. He gave her a warning glance. "I'm not saying I accept them as fact. But it throws suspicion on all that has been happening at Shorecliff."

Doris spoke up sharply, "She mustn't stay on there, Inspector."

"Perhaps not." The inspector turned to Anita again. "You asked me to look into the background of the medium, Mary Vane. I talked with the authorities in Boston. She's been operating as a spiritualist there for some years and she has not officially been in any trouble."

"Then you'd say she is genuinely able to contact the dead?" Anita said.

"No," he told her. "I'm saying she's never had trouble with the police."

"It's Anita's husband," Doris protested. "He's plotting against her!"

The inspector eyed Anita. "What do you say to that?"

"I don't know!"

"Have you any idea what the people of Shorecliff think of you?" he asked grimly. "I'll tell you, Mrs. Shore. I've talked to them all. They say it's you who must be losing your mind and not your husband!"

Doris exclaimed, "Naturally they told you that. They're trying to hurt her."

Anita studied the inspector with perplexed eyes. "Why should they tell you that?"

The inspector regarded her in stony silence. "It could be true," he said at last. "All the people I spoke with insisted you were temperamental, jealous and given to hysteria."

"Charles wouldn't say that!"

"He didn't say anything," Inspector Decker admitted. "But he didn't protest what he heard some of the others tell me. He could have." He paused. "You have only one champion among all those at Shorecliff. And that's Gordon Morehouse. He blames your husband for all the trouble."

She warmed at this information about Gordon. Of course she could have counted on his defending her. And he had been the only one! But would his word count against that of all the others? The news that Charles had shown silence when he

280

should have come to her support was especially bitter.

The inspector now stared at her sternly. "Mrs. Shore, did you lately buy a gun in Dover?"

This time she was shocked. "No!" she gasped.

"I warn you to tell the truth," he said. "Are you certain you didn't buy the gun and forget about it?"

"Do you think I'd be likely to do that?" she asked angrily.

"About two weeks ago a woman giving your name and answering your description, blonde with dark sun glasses, purchased a gun from a dealer in Dover."

There was a stunned silence.

Doris looked at her with anguish. "I wanted to warn you," she said.

She showed amazement. "But that's ridiculous! If I planned to buy a gun and keep it a secret I wouldn't deliberately give my right name."

"You might if you were in an unstable mental state," the inspector said.

"I see," she said quietly, aware the snare was closing in on her.

"Do you have a gun, Mrs. Shore?"

She hesitated before replying. She couldn't answer this without implicating

Gordon, the one person who had defended her. And she daren't do that without at least warning him first. No doubt Charles would tell the inspector about the gun soon enough. Let him find out from Charles!

She said, "I don't have the gun you refer to, Inspector. I didn't buy any gun." It was a carefully worded reply in which she hadn't denied having a weapon from another source. She hoped it would satisfy him.

It seemed to. He sat back in his chair. "If that's so," he said, "some woman has gone to the trouble of impersonating you and purchasing the gun in your name."

Doris Benson suggested, "Pat Shore or Mary Vane?" And she added, "Probably the same one is also playing the role of Amanda's ghost."

"A possibility," he agreed. And to Anita, "Do you want to remain at Shorecliff, knowing this?"

"If I leave now the truth may never be known," she said. "Is that all, Inspector?"

"For the present," he said, his stern eyes meeting hers. "You have my phone number if you feel you want to get in touch with me."

When she and Doris were alone on the

sidewalk her friend's face showed chagrin. "I thought I had won him over to your side. But he's so aloof. I don't think I did any good at all."

"Of course you did," Anita said. "But this business of someone impersonating me and buying that gun has made him doubtful about everything."

"And I'm due back in Maine to join the others," Doris said unhappily.

Anita mustered a smile for her. "Please go and don't worry. It will be all right."

With this and other hastily summoned assurances she finally convinced Doris there was no need to further interrupt her vacation. She saw her friend off and then went back to her own car. She drove swiftly to Gordon's antique shop, anxious to tell him about her interview with the inspector.

But when she got there the gawky youth who acted as Gordon's assistant told her, "Mr. Morehouse has gone to Portland to attend a sale. He won't be back until late." His pimply face took on an expectant smile. "Anything I can do?"

She shook her head. "No. You can tell him I was asking for him."

She drove on back to Shorecliff in a troubled and dismal state of mind. The interview with the inspector had not been encouraging. There had been a change in the weather to match her mood. The sun had vanished and it was now cloudy and humid. A silence hung in the air, hinting of an approaching storm.

Anita quietly let herself into the house and hurried up the shadowed stairway to her room. The weird calm continued and the sky grew darker. Standing by the screen of her open window she could hear the pounding of the waves on the beach with an awesome clarity.

Dinner was an ordeal for her. There had been no word from Gordon so she guessed he hadn't returned yet. Charles was looking very unwell and drinking too much. Pat avoided talking to her. The candles on the dining room table cast a flickering light and the rumble of a distant storm could be heard to create an eerie mood in the dark wood-paneled room. The storm which had been threatening seemed likely to break soon.

Anita left the table first and hurried out of the room. She was on her way upstairs when Charles called out to her. She halted and turned to look down at his handsome, weary face. "Yes?" she said.

"What about that gun?"

"I'd rather not discuss it."

"Would you rather I brought the police into this?" The thunder rumbled again. Closer this time.

She said. "Do what you like."

He hesitated and seemed to sway a little. "We're having a seance. I'd like you to take part."

"No," she said firmly. "And don't ask me again." And she hurried on upstairs.

She'd barely reached her room when the rain came down in great torrents. She rushed to her window and closed it. Now the thunder was loud and the lightning came in blinding blue flashes. With a tiny shiver she turned from the window. Lightning storms always terrified her.

The storm raged all evening. As she changed into her nightgown and robe she wondered if they had held the seance during this wild convulsion of nature. After she'd gotten into bed the storm ebbed and settled down to an all night rain. She had retrieved the gun from its hiding place and now had it safely hidden under her pillow. Knowing it was there gave her the courage to turn out the lights and attempt to sleep.

But the rest that came to her was tormented. It was filled with weird dreams revolving around the dead Amanda. The lovely murderess with the porcelain face seemed to emerge from her portrait and stand before her. Coming close to the bed Amanda held out a cold bony hand and touched Anita's cheek. With a frantic scream Anita shrank back from this touch of the grave.

And at the same moment she came fully awake to see the door of her bedroom swing open and Charles stumble into the room. The dim light from the hallway outlined his figure and cast a faint glow of yellow in the bedroom. Automatically she reached for the weapon under her pillow and pointed it at him.

Her husband stood there with an expression of dull bewilderment she had never seen before. Charles must have finally taken leave of his senses. He stared at her as if he intended to kill her — as well he might! Leaning against the pillow, she said tensely, "Don't come any closer!"

But Charles came a step toward her, the same malevolent expression on his face. Then he lunged forward to grasp her. It was more than she could take. In a wild effort to stop him she aimed the gun at the ceiling and fired. He halted and stared at her with those crazed eyes. And then Charles quickly collapsed and lay stretched out motionless on the bedside rug.

Anita closed her eyes and sobbed with relief.

But the moment of tearful gratitude was abruptly ended by a new horror. The air was suddenly filled with the familiar odor of the Attar of Roses and she opened her eyes to see the black-shrouded figure of Amanda. The glowing enamel face was emerging from the shadows of the far corner of the room. It came slowly toward her and she knew what she must do!

Aiming the gun at the phantom she pressed the trigger. A shot rang out and she fired again. The thing in black hesitated and then slumped down on the floor. Anita screamed and dropped the gun.

There was pounding on the door leading from the hallway and the sounds of excited voices out there. She sat in the nearly complete darkness, too dazed to do anything. It came to her that the door had been opened by Charles when he came in. Either he or the phantom must have locked it. Still numb in mind and body she ignored the knocking and shouts. At last she reached for the bedside lamp and turned it on. Charles still lay close to the bed where he'd fallen. But it was the distant crumpled figure in black who interested her most.

She got out of bed and advanced fearfully toward it.

Its back was toward her. She forced herself to kneel and touch the figure's shoulder and roll it over. As she did the weird porcelain mask was revealed and fell away to show it was nothing more than a false-face.

But it was the face under it that shocked her to alertness!

The wan, pinched face of Gordon Morehouse!

"Gordon!" she gasped.

The sound of her voice apparently reached the wounded man. His eyelids flickered and then he opened his eyes and stared up at her. A faint, bitter smile played about his thin lips.

"Always the loser!" he whispered.

"You!" she said. "You've been impersonating Amanda's ghost!"

"It almost worked," he said weakly, his eyes fixed on her. "I planted the idea Charles was going mad. I could see you'd fallen for it. Then all I had to do was see the others were convinced you were the insane, hysterical one. Once I'd given you the gun I was sure you'd use it. But on Charles . . . not on me!" He coughed weakly and she saw the blood forming beside him on the carpet. It was welling from some wound that penetrated his chest area.

"Why?" she asked in a whisper. "Why?"

Then coughing over he spoke again in a low, harsh whisper, "I was second in line for Aunt Clare's money and this place. I needed it. By eliminating Charles it would all work out. I counted on you."

"How did you get in here?"

"Secret passage in cellar. Always has been between the two houses."

She glanced toward the spot where her husband lay. "What did you do to him?"

"Drugged," Gordon whispered hoarsely. "After the seance we had a drink together. I slipped the drug in his drink. Counted on you shooting him when he came in here. Instead —" he began to choke again.

This time when the coughing ended he made no effort to speak. He sank back, his eyes fixed on the ceiling. There was no suggestion of breathing from him and she guessed that he must be dead. Only then did she realize the knocking was continuing and there were voices calling out to her to open the door. Her horrified gaze still on the weird figure on the carpet, she rose slowly and backed away to the door.

She unlocked it, her eyes still fixed on

Gordon's bloodstained body. Pat, in pink dressing gown, was the first to enter. Anita gave her a solemn glance. "Call the police," she said. "Get Inspector Decker at State Headquarters in Portsmouth."

After that it was a nightmare experience. Mrs. Miller took charge of guarding the room. Anita had the still-drugged Charles taken back to his own bedroom where she and Pat waited with him. The doctor had been called along with the police.

Pat brought some tea up from the kitchen and poured her a cup and brought it over to the bedside where she was keeping her vigil. "Take this. It will do you good," the brown-haired girl said.

Anita mechanically took the cup of the hot liquid and stared at the other girl. "What about Mrs. Morehouse?" she asked. "Does she know?"

Pat nodded. "She's been told there was an accident. That's all for the present. Mary Vane is with her. She's in her own part of the house." The girl took a sip of her tea, her eyes on Anita, then she went on, "How did you guess Gordon was the phantom?"

"I didn't. I was terrified. I shot at him wildly in the darkness."

"What about Charles?"

"Gordon gave him some kind of drug. He hoped I would shoot him. He probably came up to finish the job in case I hadn't."

Pat stared at her grimly above the steaming cup. "I knew Gordon was hard up. But I didn't guess he was this desperate."

Still partly in shock, she said, "He gave me the gun! It was his gun I killed him with!"

The police arrived first. Inspector Decker spent a few minutes with her in the bedroom and then went on to view the body. She remained with Charles until the doctor came. Then she stood by while Dr. Wilson examined him.

He finally turned to her with a frown. "He's been drugged, all right. But there's more wrong with him than that. He should be in the hospital. I'll call Dover to send an ambulance."

So the nightmare was still not over!

Inspector Decker ordered her to remain in the house when the ambulance came to take Charles to the Dover hospital. The graying police official touched her arm gently and said, "There's nothing you can do. Dr. Wilson says he's in no immediate danger. They'll be taking X-rays. You'll find out soon enough."

She stood with great tears rolling down her cheeks as the ambulance rolled away in the still rainy night. Then Inspector Decker guided her into the study for a period of questioning. When she'd told him all she knew he began pacing up and down before her.

"It fits," he admitted. "There's no question he's been playing the role of phantom to push you into madness and kill your husband."

"And he almost managed it," she said with awe.

"Almost," the inspector said, halting his pacing to stand before her. "He had a knack for female impersonation. We found the blonde wig and dress he used when he went to Dover and bought that gun in your name — his first step to involve you in Charles' murder."

"But those spells I had?" she said. "What about them?"

Inspector Decker offered her a rare bitter smile. "Did you know Gordon was a diabetic?"

She frowned. "He drank orange juice and . . ."

"Yes. He took insulin to control it. He used a hypo to inject himself. And that's what he gave you when you thought the phantom was plunging a hatpin into you. You received a giant dose of insulin. Enough to induce convulsions."

Her eyes opened wide. "That explains the bruises on my arm and the soreness."

The inspector nodded grimly. "We should have listened to you then. Dr. Wilson should have spotted what was wrong. But no one was looking for anything like this. No one suspected Gordon."

"And everyone was quick to believe I was the hysterical female," she said in a dry voice.

"I'm afraid we sometimes don't show much imagination, Mrs. Shore," he admitted. "Still, we haven't done so badly."

Anita was not willing to agree to this yet she was too weary to argue. Decker ended the interview and insisted that she take some sleeping tablets and go to bed in Charles' room.

The rain had ended by morning but there was thick fog and some drizzle when she went downstairs. She was still a trifle dizzy from her drugged sleep but she had at least managed some rest. The first person she met was Mary Vane. The gauntly beautiful medium was waiting for her at the bottom of the stairs.

Anita asked, "How is Mrs. Morehouse?"

The medium shrugged. "She's not taking it too badly. I don't think there was much love lost between mother and son. Pat is with her now."

"I see," she said quietly.

"Have you had word about your husband?"

"Not yet."

"It's not liable to be good," the medium told her, the keen black eyes fixed on her. "I used my Ouija board this morning and the message spelled out Amanda and Death."

Anita shook her head angrily. "I don't want to hear anymore about such things."

The dark woman raised herself up imperiously. In her hollow voice, she said, "Yet what I say is true. Dr. Wilson doesn't know what is wrong with your husband. But I do. Amanda has cast a spell on him. He has been her puppet ever since he entered this house!"

"No!" Anita protested. "I don't want to believe that!"

"You merely killed that foolish, wicked man pretending to be a ghost last night," Mary Vane went on triumphantly. "But the true ghost remains in command here. Her curse is working against you all! And I'm the only one who can help you!"

She knew what the medium was doing! Trying to rebuild a position of strength within the house. Attempting to single her out as the next one to sponsor the seances because Mary Vane was not going to surrender a good paying thing without at least an attempt to save it. And yet there was that slim possibility the weird spiritualist was right. Charles might be lost in a spell cast by the century dead Amanda. The seance might be the only hope!

And then the phone in the hallway rang shrilly and Anita left the medium to answer it. The voice at the other end of the line belonged to Dr. Wilson. The veteran doctor sounded worried.

"The X-rays have shown what we expected," he said. "There's a large splinter of bone causing pressure on the brain. Something left over from that old injury your husband received."

"How bad is it?"

"Needs attention right away," the Doctor told her. "We're having a specialist come down from Boston this morning. Better to operate here than try to move him."

"Will he be all right?" There was a tremor in Anita's voice.

"Of course he will," Dr. Wilson assured

her. "Don't you worry about a thing."

"I won't," she said, and put down the phone. Then she turned to the medium. "They've found out Charles' trouble and they're going to operate. I'm leaving for the hospital in a few minutes. When I come back I don't want to find you here. I'm sure you understand."

Anger gleamed in the medium's eyes. "Ignore the curse if you like," she said in her hollow voice. "You will come seeking my help when you find out Amanda's evil power!" And she turned and stalked majestically upstairs.

Anita watched after her with an inner rage of her own. They had all been bullied by the medium long enough. But she had no time to worry about that now. She was only too anxious to get to Dover and be at the hospital for a report of the operation.

It was close to noon when Dr. Wilson sought her out in the waiting room. He smiled reassuringly as she rose to meet him. "It went very well," he told her. "You'll be able to see Charles in the morning. And you'll be talking to him in a few days."

She drew a great sigh of relief. "There are so many questions," she said.

He nodded. "I know. He hasn't been himself lately, has he?"

"Hardly."

"With that pressure on his brain, no wonder. It would be bound to make him irritable and might cause a complete personality change." He smiled. "Well, no matter. He'll be all right now."

Anita discovered this to be true a few days later when she and Charles had their first long talk. The bandages that covered all his head made his handsome face look thinner and paler than before. But his old smile had returned and his eyes no longer held that wild gleam.

"I don't know what happened to me," he said. "When I first arrived at Shorecliff I felt pretty well. Of course I worried about you and that ghost business. I had an idea Pat and Gordon might be working something together. They had almost been engaged. That's why I decided to pretend to be deeply interested in her."

"When you began working on your Amanda book you were with her almost all the time," Anita reminded him.

"I know," he said. "I was getting more confused. And I began losing my hold on reality as the pressure built from that bone splinter. I was lost!"

She patted his hand. "At least we've found you again."

But he still had weeks to face in hospital. And these were weeks with meaning for Anita and all the others at Shorecliff. Mary Vane left the day of the operation and was not heard from again. Inspector Decker did all he could to keep the scandal of Gordon Morehouse's death at a minimum. As the weeks went by it was soon forgotten as a topic of conversation. Pat moved into the other part of the house with Aunt Clem and took over the management of Gordon's antique shop. With the fresh capital and shrewd talents she could bring to the business it was generally agreed she would make a success of it.

The day came for Charles to leave the hospital. Because he was not well enough to stand a journey to Boston she drove him back to Shorecliff. It was a pleasant sunny afternoon and the old mansion looked familiar and inviting as they halted before it.

Anita shut off the engine and looked at him. "Well, we're back," she said.

"Yes," he smiled faintly. "You don't sound too happy about it."

"Sorry," she said. "Shall we go in?"

They were met at the door by Mrs. Miller who for once offered them a smile and a friendly greeting. It seemed like a good omen. Rather than going upstairs they automatically went into the living room and stood before Amanda's portrait.

Charles stared up at the arrogant, beautiful face. "I'd like us to go on living here. But not with her. I'll send her to Boston to some art dealer."

Anita, who was also studying the painting with a thoughtful expression, shook her head. "Let's not be selfish. We have a happiness she never knew. Let her stay. I don't think she'll bother us again."

For an answer, her husband took her in his arms and kissed her tenderly.

We hope you have enjoyed this Large Print book. Other Thorndike, Wheeler or Chivers Press Large Print books are available at your library or directly from the publishers.

For more information about current and up-coming titles, please call or write, without obligation, to:

Publisher
Thorndike Press
295 Kennedy Memorial Drive
Waterville, ME   04901
Tel. (800) 223-1244

Or visit our Web site at:
www.gale.com/thorndike
www.gale.com/wheeler

OR

Chivers Large Print
published by BBC Audiobooks Ltd
St James House, The Square
Lower Bristol Road
Bath BA2 3SB
England
Tel. +44(0) 800 136919
email: bbcaudiobooks@bbc.co.uk
www.bbcaudiobooks.co.uk

All our Large Print titles are designed for easy reading, and all our books are made to last.